The Pente Force Chronicles Mind Games

By
Ann Marie R. Harvie

Out of This World
PUBLISHING

The Pente Force Chronicles: Mind Games

Copyright ©2020 Ann Marie R. Harvie

Cover Design:
Acharya Hargreaves -
www.acharyahargreaves.com

Interior illustrations:
Brian D. Murphy - brian@parttimedesign.com

Editor: Brian Harvie
Proofreader: Sally Rigione
Beta Reader: Nicole Reineke

Out of this World Publishing owned and operated by Ann Marie R. Harvie in Shrewsbury, Massachusetts
http://www.penteforce.com

Follow Ann Marie R. Harvie on Twitter: @EditorYE, Facebook: https://www.facebook.com/PenteForce or on Word Press: https://storiesfromoutofthisworld.wordpress.com

ISBN: 978-0-578-65460-7

Library of Congress Control Number: 2020903719

Published in the United States

First Printing: March 2020

Table of Contents

Acknowledgements

Thank you...

...to Brian, Sally and Nicole for taking a piece of coal and creating a diamond.

...to Rachel, Ryan and Odin for understanding when Mom needed to write.

This book is dedicated to Junior, Denny, Laurie and Tori. And to Randy – as Charlie you will live forever.

Introduction

"Freeze!" Star ordered.

Both of her hands were on her Ks-99 as she crouched down close to the wall of the starfighter to dodge any incoming laser fire. It was dark inside the cabin and her eyes had to adjust to the lack of light. A death-like silence filled the chamber. She caught a sudden movement in the corner of her eye and turned her head. Her eyes quickly became accustomed to the dark and she was able to see shapes inside the cabin. A shadowed figure leaned over a couch. As she watched, it yanked up another figure to a sitting position.

"Lights!" she barked to the cabin's computer.

The voice-activated computer complied and the lights came on. Star saw the face of her enemy. Freckles lightly sprinkled the alabaster skin. Fire-red hair flowed in thick waves down to the young woman's shoulders. Her bright green eyes blazed with anger.

It took a moment for the intruder's face to register in Star's mind. When it did, she couldn't believe her eyes. *Tessa.* But that was impossible. Star was told she fell eight months ago during the battle against Wardon on the planet Mars. The intruder's eyes widened for just a moment and Star knew that she recognized her as well.

"Tessa?" whispered Star, almost to herself.

Hatred flashed in Tessa's eyes as they narrowed into tiny green slits.

Star felt as if she had just been punched in the stomach. Tessa had been one of her closest friends. Why was a Federation Knight and the daughter of a highly decorated general working for Wardon? Despite her disbelief, Star remained in her attack stance, her weapon aimed directly between Tessa's eyes.

"Surrender," she ordered.

Star struggled to keep her emotions from surfacing. Her heart raced as her confusion and disbelief began to consume her. Was this her enemy? Should she shoot the woman with whom she'd been through so much? Memories flooded her mind of battles where the two fought side-by-side. For the first time in her military career, Star, the Federation's best, didn't know what to do.

Tessa's face revealed an internal battle of her own. She seemed to be struggling to keep her angry expression; she also seemed to be fighting back tears. "Back off, Star," said Tessa with a choked voice. "Leave now and I'll let you live."

Star stayed in position, her Ks-99 never wavering. "I said surrender, traitor."

Tessa blinked as if she'd been smacked out of a trance. "I'm not a traitor," she replied in a shaky voice. Her expression softened and the hate in her eyes gradually faded. "Whatever you think right now, Star, I'm not a traitor."

Star could not will her heart to stop slamming against her chest. She struggled unsuccessfully to steady her breathing. Her hands, while still on her gun, were cold and clammy. She battled with herself to keep them steady. She didn't want to believe her eyes, but facts were facts. "You are a Wardon assassin and a traitor."

Tessa's voice was urgent, her expression panicked. "I'm not! I don't want to do this. I have to."

An explanation for the bizarre situation suddenly popped into Star's head. Of course! She wasn't doing this of her own free will. She was being *made* to kill for them. "You can surrender. You don't have to kill for them anymore. I can help you."

10

Tessa's eyes watered and her breathing quickened. Her gaze darted around the room as if she was in a hurry. "I can't surrender, Star. You can't help me. I'm not the old Tessa," she said in a soft whisper. Tears began to stream down her face. "I've been changed. Turn around and leave now. You're not the one I'm after."

Star furrowed her brows in confusion. She took a step toward her friend.

"Stay back!" Tessa ordered angrily as she nudged her blaster against the unconscious leader's head. "What do you mean changed? I don't understand."

Tessa's face paled. She blinked her eyes hard as if to focus them and shook her head. Her breathing came in quick shallow breaths as she explained to Star the horror of her capture on Mars by the enemy. Wardon's methods of torture were excruciating and Tessa was caught each time she attempted suicide.

"They tortured me, Star," she said in an agonized tone. "Oh God, it was pure hell."

Tessa continued her horrifying story, describing how the Wardon scientists had implanted an organic mind-control device in her brain through her nose. She said she could feel it wrap around her brain as it grew. When the Wardons gave her orders, the worm made sure she obeyed. It would inflict a pain so great Tessa would almost go insane and would have to comply.

"I can help, Tessa," said Star. "Just put the gun down. We're not far from a Federation base. We can get that thing out of your head."

Tessa let out a frustrated breath. The white around her green eyes began to turn pink. "You don't understand! I must finish my mission!"

Once again, hatred flashed in Tessa's green eyes and Star knew the thing in her head was taking over. Star didn't know what to do. She could not release Tessa. Duty had to come first.

"Let me help you, Tessa. I'm still your friend. Please trust me."

Tessa took a deep breath and let it out. Her expression changed from angry to sad. It seemed that for the moment she had won the battle for her mind. She gazed at her friend for what seemed like forever. Sweat beaded on Tessa's forehead as her breath quickened. "Star, no matter what, you can't let my father and sisters think I am a traitor," she said as she placed her blaster against her temple.

"Tessa don't," shouted Star.

Before she could pull the trigger to end her life, Tessa's face contorted as if in horrible pain. She screamed in agony and blood trickled from her nose. With one hand, she grabbed her own head while she tried to pull the laser's trigger with the other. "Leave me alone!" she screamed. "I'm not going to do it!"

Star didn't know what command the thing in Tessa's head was giving, but she couldn't stand the torture her friend's agony. Concern

13

for Tessa overruled caution and Star lowered her weapon. She moved toward her friend to help her.

Tessa let go of her head and straightened. Blood red sclera circled the green pupils. Her face contorted into a maniacal expression. The mind control had taken over. Star's heart sank. Tessa pointed her blaster at Star, though it shook violently in her hand. She squeezed her eyes shut and let out a cry of agony. "No!" she screamed at the ceiling. "I'm not killing for you anymore!"

Tessa grabbed her right arm with her left hand as she desperately fought to control herself. She was able to jerk the gun enough to prevent a fatal shot, but it went off just the same and shot Star in the right arm. Star fell back.

Star's many years of intensive training took over. She felt only enough pain in her to command her brain to act. She jumped to her feet in an attack position. Her left hand rose, and shot Tessa in the chest before she had time to think about it. She instantly regretted what she did.

"Tessa!" she cried as the redhead fell to the floor behind the couch. Star stumbled to her friend's side to see a pool of blood quickly forming on the floor.

Tessa's face went translucent from the loss of blood. She flashed a smile at Star; death was imminent and she seemed at peace. Soon there would be no more pain. Tears streamed down Star's face. Had she not attacked, Star could have saved Tessa; she just knew it.

"Tessa! I'm so sorry. I didn't mean to!" she cried.

"It's okay. There was no other way. I wouldn't let it take over. I couldn't kill my dearest friend," Tessa wheezed.

The bloodstain on the carpet grew at a rapid rate. Star tried to apply pressure to the wound, but try as she might Star could not save her friend. "I'm not a traitor. I killed because I couldn't control myself. I love the Chain of Life and I love my father, you know that."

Tessa's body convulsed and Star cradled her friend in her arms. "I know. It's not your fault. I'll tell him," she said.

Tessa said nothing else. Her body shook once more and became still. Star brought her friend home to her heartbroken family. She explained repeatedly what happened, giving General Hunter and his remaining daughters all the information she could give them. She had hoped that they would understand – that she had no choice, that she didn't want to do what she did. Her hope was dashed -- Tessa's family turned on Star and blamed her for their loved one's death, the mind control device seemingly forgotten. General Hunter did not believe Star and made her board his Warship the HORIZON to tell her story every year so that he could catch her in a lie and send her to prison forever for what she had done to his little girl. Every year they found themselves facing each other in a small interrogation room on the HORIZON. Every year Star would tell her story. And every year the questioning always ended in General Hunter screaming at Star and calling her a murderer. Star could have refused to submit to the abuse, but inside she felt she deserved it. She DID kill Tessa; it didn't matter whether it was an accident or not. She was dead and never coming back to her family. She hated every moment of it, but she would continue to come when summoned until he finally believed her.

Mind Games – Part 1

Star sat in the cramped interrogation room aboard the Federation Defense Warship, HORIZON. The weight of the stale air in the room caused her to take in a deep breath now and again as she waited to be questioned. The cold steel of the chair began to penetrate her uniform and she tried not to shiver. Noises of shouting and people walking back and forth outside the room filtered in from under the door. Star avoided looking at the double-sided mirror that hung in front of her. She stayed as still as she could, giving no show to those who may be behind it. Instead she stared down at the small, stainless steel table in front of her.

Every year for the last five years she endured sitting in an interrogation room for hours answering the same questions about the same thing. Yet, she didn't fight the annual order. She knew she could file a complaint of harassment, but she never did. She always came when ordered and went through the same hell every time. She felt it was her penance.

Star knew General William Hunter would be walking through the door at any moment. He would come in, glare at her, throw down his tablet and begin the hours of seemingly endless questions. Every year he would ask them and every year she would give him the same answers, never once changing her story. There was nothing to change – it was the absolute truth. Yet, he refused to believe it. He refused to believe the account Star gave about the day she killed her best friend. The day Star killed his daughter.

As Star sat in the chair, her mind went back to the day when her friend Tessa, a Federation Knight thought killed in battle, pointed a laser at her and fired. Star dodged the blast and fired back, killing her. This was all just after Star discovered Tessa was an assassin for Wardon. An assassin under a vicious mind control method that once implanted could not be removed. Still, Tessa was her best friend, and many wondered if there really wasn't any way to bring her in alive. Star let out a long breath when she thought about what the mind control had done to Tessa and what it forced Star to do to defend herself.

Star came back to the present when the door handle to the interrogation room moved and the door clicked open. Star's eyes furrowed when she didn't see General Hunter, but her childhood friend Dr. Jared Thomas walk through the door. "Jared? What are you doing here? You better leave. General Hunter will be here any minute," she said.

"He's already here," barked an older, gruff voice from behind the young doctor.

The large, daunting figure of General Hunter filled the frame of the door as Jared took his place in front of the table to Star's left. General Hunter did not look like a man in his late 50's. Although his military cropped hair was pure white, his tall stature and broad shoulders made him seem like an imposing younger man. There was a time when Star could remember thinking no one looked more like a general than he did. Now she had trouble looking at him. His big green eyes reminded her of Tessa. Star silently eyed the two men and waited for General Hunter to slam down his tablet on the table, signaling the beginning of a very long day. However, he didn't slam the tablet – he held it tight in his hands. An uncomfortable silence filled the room. Star began to wish the General would start yelling.

He didn't yell. For the longest time, he said nothing. Jared was the one who began to ask questions. "Star, General Hunter invited me to this... well ... interview so I could ask you some very specific questions about what happened the day Tessa Hunter died."

For the first time, she noticed Jared had a notebook. Star tried not to show her confusion. What was going on? "Of course," she said. "I'll answer anything you like."

Jared gave his friend a grim nod. "Thank you. I have notes from past recorded interviews. Now, when you first saw Major Tessa Hunter, you said she looked as she always did when you knew her?"

"Yes."

"Her movements did not appear jerky?"

"No, not when we first had our confrontation. At the end... when she was struggling to try to regain control, her muscles did begin to jerk."

"And her eyes? You said at the beginning, her eyes appeared normal?"

"Yes, her eyes were a bright green, just like General Hunter's."

General Hunter glared at Star, but said nothing. He listened intently to Jared's questions.

"And at the end?"

"At the end, the whites of her eyes turned red, as if blood were filling them."

23

"Do you believe that is when the mind control device completely took over?"

Star shook her head. "I don't know. It was all so sudden and the shock of having her in front of me when we all thought she was dead. At first, I thought she was a traitor working for Wardon, but then when she told me about the mind control device in her head..."

General Hunter whirled around and slapped the wall with the palms of his hands with a loud, angry grunt. Star knew her remarks were hurtful, but she wanted to tell the truth – again – about what happened that day. Jared, the odd man in the room, seemed intrigued by this information and ignored the general's outburst. "I wonder," he said to the general, who was still red-faced with rage. "I wonder if we can find a way."

The general turned to Jared. "That's why you're here, Dr. Thomas. I know there is a way and you can find it."

Star's eyes went from one man to the other. What was all this? What was going on?

24

What was Jared looking for? Jared stood up. As if he suddenly remembered she was in the room, he turned to Star. "General Hunter has an idea. He thinks we can find a way to eliminate the mind control devices from their victims without killing them in the process," he said. "We want to find a way to save our soldiers and the rest of Wardon's mind control victims."

The Special Forces commander's eyebrows went up, but she said nothing. She knew Jared well and she knew he would elaborate more if she waited long enough. Jared put one of his hands on his hips and the other scratched his chin as he paced the small room. "You see, these worms are organic. They wrap themselves around the brain stem and the spinal cord becoming one with its host as they grow. Wardon has a way of communicating with them. Possibly with a smaller device they insert into the worm before they infect the victim. There might be a way to kill the worm and surgically remove it while keeping the brain stem and spinal cord intact, but we'd have to have a live specimen to experiment on," he said. "You see, once the host dies, the worm dies. It practically disintegrates and leaves no researchable evidence."

"That's where you come in, Commander," snarled the general.

Now Star's eyebrows furrowed. Were they asking her to have one implanted inside her? "Sir?"

"We need a live victim with a mind control device in their body," he said. "We need you to get us one."

Star's confusion mounted. "I'm sorry, I don't understand. I don't know where to get one of these victims for you to experiment on."

"Ah!" said Jared bursting with excitement. "That's easy. There are plenty of them on Dyanzia."

Star could feel her jaw drop. "Dyanzia? That's been a Wardon-occupied planet for decades now. You know that, General. Wardons will be swarming all over that planet."

"Actually, no," said General Hunter. "We have intelligence that verifies that because it has been so long since they conquered the planet and because the Federation Chain of Life made no effort to liberate it, it's now a planet where Tozar keeps his supply of zombie slaves. Dyanzians under his mind control are hardly a security risk. There is a small presence, but we're not talking an army."

Star stared at the two men in front of her. "So, you want us to go in there and get you a Dyanzian zombie?"

"There is no us. Your team will not be joining you. This assignment is for you and one other," said General Hunter.

Star glanced at Jared and recalled the last mission she went on with him. "I'm not taking Dr. Thomas on a mission like this," she declared.

"Not Dr. Thomas. He'll be busy preparing for the Dyanzian's arrival. No, you will be accompanied by Major Brianna Hunter."

Star could feel the blood drain from her face. "You're youngest daughter? *That* Brianna?"

General Hunter straightened. "Major Hunter is a decorated Federation Knight, as her sister was before you killed her. She is as committed to this endeavor as I am."

Star rose from her chair, disbelief fixed solidly on her face. "Sir, this mission is REALLY dangerous. There's a good chance no one will come back alive. Do you really want to risk her? I'll go alone if you don't want my team to come and I'll find your zombie."

General Hunter straightened. "This is not up for negotiation. Major Hunter is going on this mission and that is final."

Star let out a heavy sigh and shot Jared a dubious look. "Okay, so we're going to Dyanzia. What's the plan?"

"I've had a shuttle retrofitted to suit the needs of this mission," said General Hunter. "The HORIZON will take you as far as the edge of the Dyanzian System. Monitors have detected a blind spot in the surveillance system. You're on your own to fly in through the spot. Find a zombie, bring it back and get home. Simple as that."

Jared began to pace again and began talking with his hands as he spoke. "Now the shuttle will have a cage for the zombie and there will be a tranquilizer on board as well as a black hood. The tranquilizer should knock out the zombie for the entire trip, but we know very little about Dyanzian physiology. I would suggest you try to tranquilize him or her as soon as possible and then immediately put the hood on so he or she can't see anything. If it sees too much for too long, there's a chance that it can report back to the Wardons. That could be disastrous both for you and the mission."

Jared did not make Star feel any better about taking Brianna on the mission. "Mr. Sanderson signed off on this?" she asked.

"He did."

The general's answer surprised Star. She wondered how much he told Mr. Sanderson about his plan. She tugged at the left sleeve of her uniform and sighed again. "Okay then. Let's do this. When do we leave?"

"We are already on our way. The coordinates were set the moment you came on board. It will take about a day at top speed to get there. You've been assigned a cabin. An extra uniform and other necessities are in a backpack in Logistics. You can pick it up when you get your cabin assignment. Get a good night's rest. You're going to need it," said General Hunter.

She nodded to Jared and saluted the General who dismissed her. Star shook her head as she walked to Logistics to get her bag and assigned cabin. *They're crazy*, she thought, *and there's a good chance somebody won't be coming home from this.*

***

The next day, Star slowly approached the small shuttle in the hangar bay. She dreaded this mission – one she believed was designed for her not to return.

It was time to go. The HORIZON was on the edge of the Dyanzia System. It was as close as it could get without being detected. Star and Brianna would have to go the rest of the way in the shuttle. Not even the whining of engines could drown out Star's troubled thoughts about the mission.

As Star approached the shuttle, she instantly recognized Brianna's face. She was the image of her sister, only with blonde hair. She had the same bright green eyes famous with the Hunter clan. Brianna's eyes blazed with hate as she looked up at Star from the flight checklist she had been going over with one of the hangar crew. Star went over and over in her mind how she wanted to deal with the impending, awkward situation of meeting Brianna again, and found no good solution.

She stopped just a foot or so from Brianna and stared back at her with authoritative eyes. She gave the young woman a slight nod. "Major," she greeted with a commanding tone.

31

Out of the corner of Star's eye she noticed the hangar attendant stood with his mouth slightly agape. Everyone knew Star's disastrous fall from grace with the Hunter family – she was sure the mission would elicit plenty of talk. Star turned her attention back to Brianna when she heard a curt, "Commander," come from her direction.

Star stuck her hand out for the checklist. Brianna silently handed it to her. Star quickly scanned all the green check marks indicating the shuttle and the equipment passed inspection. "All set then?" she asked the hangar attendant as she shoved the checklist in his hands.

She didn't wait for an answer. "Let's go," she said to Brianna as she walked past her into the shuttle.

Star sat in the pilot's seat and strapped herself in. When she heard Brianna's footsteps behind her, she began preparations for takeoff. "Major, did you familiarize yourself with the equipment we'll be working with on this mission?"

"Yes, Ma'am. The cage is strong and the hood's material is impenetrable to light but still breathable."

Star did not look back. She listened as the hatch of the shuttle door hissed shut and locked with a quick click. The shuttle only had enough room for two seats, a short walkway to the back of the shuttle, a bathroom, a small weapons room and a supply room. The station crew removed all the weapons and shelving to make room for a cage large enough to hold one 8-foot tall Dyanzian. A tranquilizer gun was the only remaining firearm. All the two women had for real firepower were their own laser guns. Most of the supply room was taken up with an extra fuel tank that would guarantee them enough fuel to get back to the HORIZON.

Brianna sat down in the seat next to Star and buckled herself in. "I can fly if you wish," she said flatly.

"No, I want to fly," said Star as she punched the radio to signal they were ready.

"Send us out," she ordered.

After hearing a garbled "Yes, Ma'am," on the other end of the radio, the shuttle rotated 180 degrees then slowly pushed forward to the bay entrance. Once the shuttle was in place, a green light flashed on the outside wall of the hangar, indicating the shield was down and they were cleared to go. Star punched the control buttons and the shuttle left the bay on its way to Dyanzia.

Star entered the coordinates to Dyanzia into the shuttle's navigation system and turned to Brianna. "Okay, so this is how it's going to go – we get in, get the Dyanzian, we get out. I'm in charge and you follow my orders," she said.

"Sounds simple enough," Brianna responded dryly.

"It's only simple if you do exactly as I say. I've been doing missions like this for a long time. You're a squad leader for the Federation

Knights and have been sitting in a 55-ton laser tank for five years."

Brianna's eyes narrowed. "Are you saying I'm not qualified?"

"I'm saying you are not trained for this job."

"I'll get the job done and I'll do it for my sister."

A short time passed before Brianna added, "You know, she was his favorite."

Star felt a chill go through her. "Yes," she said flatly.

"When I was younger, I thought the two of you were so amazing. I wanted to be just like you," Brianna continued.

Star's heart sank, but she tried not to let it show on her face. She kept her eyes straight, staring out the shuttle window and not making eye contact. "Please tell me you're not on this mission so you could have alone time with me to tell me you hate me," she said, trying hard not to show emotion.

Brianna did not show Star the same courtesy. Her head snapped in Star's direction, and although Star didn't look, she could almost feel the heat coming from the young major's rage. "I do hate you. My whole family hates you. I wish you were dead instead of her. I wish that you let her kill you that day. None of us believe for a minute there was nothing you could do to save her. How could you? How could you do that to her? You were like our sister. You were our sister and we TRUSTED you."

Brianna's words cut deep, but again, Star kept calm. The mission ahead was dangerous and she had to stay in authority. She took a moment to make sure she could speak in a steady voice. "It won't be today or tomorrow, but someday I hope you'll know that everything I have ever told your family has been true. Now, we are on a dangerous mission in honor of Tessa. I expect you to remember that I am your commander and that you will obey me until this is over."

"Yes, Ma'am," Brianna hissed.

Star did not continue the conversation. She didn't want to spend the rest of the trip fighting. A cold, uncomfortable silence filled the shuttle for the duration of the trip. Star felt relieved when Dyanzia appeared on the viewing screen. She shut down the radio and any equipment that could register on Wardon tracking instruments and steered toward the small window of space identified by Federation Defense. When they entered the atmosphere, Star cut the main engines and flew silently through the Dyanzian night sky utilizing the auxiliary engines.

While Star flew, Brianna watched the heat sensing radar to find Dyanzians moving about in a forested area of the planet. All the heavily populated areas would be filled with Wardon soldiers and scientists. Reports from Federation Intelligence were that Dyanzians under mind control could wander freely about the planet as they could be called back if needed.

After a few minutes, Star heard Brianna take in a quick breath of excitement. She jammed her finger onto the radar screen. "There! I see two of them. Just a few hundred feet away."

"We only need one," Star said.

She would rather find one alone than risk the other one seeing them and blowing their cover.

"Then we'll only take one. We'll stun them both, but just take one."

Star shook her head. "Try to find a lone heat signature."

Brianna let out a frustrated sigh. After a moment, she ran her hand roughly through her curly blonde hair. "Look, I want to get this done as quickly as possible so we can get home, don't you?"

Star opened her mouth to order Brianna to obey her, but stopped herself. Of course she wanted this done, but confronting two zombies was a risk. Brianna was an unaltered human and wouldn't be much use in a hand-to-hand confrontation with a Dyanzian. Against her better judgement, however, she relented and landed the shuttle close to the two heat signatures.

"Get the cage ready!" ordered Star once they landed. Brianna quickly moved to the back of the shuttle and opened the cage and unraveled the belts. She also took the hood, restraints and tranquilizer and met Star at the shuttle door. Star took the gun and the restraints. She pointed a finger at the junior officer. "I'll shoot and put on the restraints, you put the bag over its head," she said. "Stay with me at all times. DO NOT leave my side!"

"Yes, Ma'am," said Brianna.

The two Soldiers stood at the entrance and looked around their surroundings before stepping out. Brianna pulled out a small heat sensor and began to scan the area for signatures. After turning about 50 degrees, something flashed on the screen. "There's one just a few dozen yards away," she whispered.

Star nodded and began walking in the direction Brianna indicated. Brianna was right next to her. "Keep a look out for the other one," Star whispered.

There were two, which meant the other Dyanzian was shambling around in the night undetected by the hand scanner. That was a problem. Although the heat scanner wasn't detecting the other one, it could be anywhere. The new turn of events was exactly why Star didn't want to follow two signatures.

Soon Star heard feet shuffling towards them. She signaled for Brianna to shut off the heat sensor and follow her. The two darted behind a large bush and waited. Moments later, a male Dyanzian in ragged clothes stumbled past them. Star's eyes quickly adjusted to the dark. In the moonlight she could see he was a young man, his eyes glossed over as if he were sleepwalking. His eyes and his stiff gait told the Special Forces commander that he had been infected a long time ago. Star felt a chill go through her. The Dyanzian stood close to 8 feet tall and was well-built. Dyanzians were known for super human strength. If anything went wrong, he could easily tear them apart with his bare hands.

Star waited for the Dyanzian to go past before she aimed and fired. Almost immediately, he dropped with a soft thud. The two soldiers were on him in moments, with Brianna putting the black hood over his head and Star securing the restraints on his hands. Brianna sized up the Dyanzian with an amazed "whoa" and it became apparent the Federation Knight had never seen a Dyanzian up close.

"This guy is huge!"

Star didn't answer Brianna. She grabbed one arm and began to drag the Dyanzian towards the shuttle. Brianna followed Star's lead and took the other arm to assist. With both dragging him, it was easier to load the Dyanzian zombie on the ship and place him in the cage. Star left Brianna to strap their captive into the cage, while she ran to the cockpit to take off.

They were barely off the ground when Star felt two hands around her throat. She suddenly realized the other Dyanzian they were tracking somehow got into the shuttle. Her mind raced. It must've gone in the bathroom or the weapons room in the back while they were capturing the other one. The hands around Star's throat restricted her windpipe, so she couldn't yell for help. The zombie pulled her back in her chair so she could not control the shuttle or activate the autopilot. The last thing Star remembered was feeling the shuttle spin out of control.

***

Star woke slowly to an ever-increasing pain in her head, the smell of smoke and the sound of Brianna grunting as she avoided the grasp of the growling, snarling Dyanzian zombie. Star struggled to get up. Brianna didn't have the strength to beat her opponent – if she didn't keep moving, the Dyanzian would have no trouble killing her. Star shook her head to help refocus her vision before she could stand up and assist Brianna. The two combatants clutched at each other, then the Dyanzian started throwing Brianna all over the cabin. The Dyanzian struggling with Brianna was a tall, heavy set woman. She had to be the other Dyanzian they saw on the radar.

Star pulled out her Ks-99 laser, but with her blurry vision she couldn't get a clear shot of the zombie. The Dyanzian had Brianna by her throat and Brianna had the Dyanzian by the hair. Star tried to pry the two apart, but the Dyanzian broke her hold on Brianna and grabbed Star. She soon felt herself flying to the opposite end of the cabin, hitting the wall and banging her already injured head.

A white light flashed from behind Star's eyes, temporarily blinding her. By some miracle, she held on to her weapon. Brianna and the Dyanzian zombie continued to struggle. Star could hear Brianna gasping for breath as the Dyanzian began to choke the life out her. Star fought to get up and tried to shake her vision back. Once she regained her eyesight well enough to distinguish one from the other, Star aimed her weapon and fired. The laser found its mark and the Dyanzian fell dead on the shuttle floor, her weight taking Brianna down with her. The Federation Knight coughed several times before getting out from under the dead Dyanzian. Once Brianna was out of danger, Star sank to the floor, her strength spent. She closed her eyes and put her head between her legs to fight the intense nausea that threatened to cause her to vomit. Brianna crawled to Star, still trying to get her breath. "Are you all right?" she gasped.

Star lifted her head, her eyes still closed. "We have to see if this will fly. The Wardons probably heard the crash. If we can't get it to fly, we've got to get out of here."

Brianna, still coughing, nodded and hurried to the controls to see if the engine would start. The engine moaned and several alarms sounded. Brianna let out a string of obscenities and slammed her hands on the panel. Star could hear Brianna's footsteps approach. She felt

Brianna's arms slip under her shoulders and lift her up. "We've got to go," she said, her voice urgent and breathy. Star felt Brianna drag her to the hatch. Star could hear the muffled growls of the other zombie. She tried to walk on her own and stumbled with the effort. Her head exploded in excruciating pain. Brianna continued to help her and soon Star could feel the cool night air on her face. Brianna pulled her into some bushes and sat her down. "Star, how bad are you hurt?" she asked urgently.

Before Star could answer, she heard the rustling of branches in the bushes behind her. She felt Brianna stand up and heard her firearm leave its holster. "Stay back!" Star heard her order to someone behind her.

"We can help you," said a man's baritone voice respond in broken Universal. "We need to hurry. They'll be here soon."

Star heard another male voice in her ear as she felt herself being lifted by abnormally large, muscled arms. "It's okay, we're friends."

The commander's body stiffened. She felt

weak and nauseous. She could not open her eyes without everything spinning. Her heart beat fast in her chest as she felt herself and the man begin to move. Her mind instantly went to her companion. "Brianna!" she called.

The man who carried her made a hushing sound and began to run faster with her as if she weighed nothing. She heard Brianna behind her telling someone she was not hurt and could run herself. The first man's voice said it would be faster if he carried her. Star realized the men had to be Dyanzians. But how was that possible?

Star felt leaves and branches touch her back and could hear breaking twigs under the Dyanzian's feet as they fled the crash site. After what seemed like forever, the man stopped running. There were other voices now speaking– some scared, some urgent. The man who carried Star transferred her to another pair of arms. Star did not understand the language the man spoke to the other Dyanzian.

"Federation warriors," he said quickly in his native tongue. "This one is badly hurt."

The new arms were strong, but smaller than the first ones. She felt the person holding her turn quickly away from the other Dyanzian. "Were you seen?" a female voice asked in broken Universal.

"No."

There was no more conversation. The woman began walking away with Star in her arms. Soon Star felt a change in air and knew she was being carried indoors. She could feel herself being lowered and then felt her body being laid down upon a hard cot. Star tried to turn on her side to get up, but the woman gently pushed her on her back. A firm but gentle voice urged her to stay still. "Just lay there for a moment so I can see what's wrong. I see much blood in your hair and around your face."

Star opened and closed her eyes to refocus them. "I hit my head during the crash and then again during a fight with a zom... with a Dyanzian under mind control," explained Star.

"I can't focus my eyes. Everything spins when I open them."

The Special Forces commander felt large, calloused hands on either side of her face gently turn it from side to side. Star instinctively opened her eyes at the touch. "That's it. Keep them opened even if things are spinning," said the woman.

Things were spinning. It wasn't long before Star felt ill. The woman saw her discomfort. "Okay, close them," said the woman.

Star quickly closed her eyes and the world stopped spinning. "I am Abia. I am the tribe elder and physician. At a minimum you have a serious concussion," she concluded. "I'm surprised you are awake at all. You need real medical attention."

"There's no time for that. My colleague and I need to get back to our shuttle," said Star.

"Why are you here? Did you crash? What are you doing on Dyanzia?"

Star kept silent. Revealing her mission, especially the part about capturing a zombie, was not something she wanted to do. "I came with another woman, where is she?"

"She is safe. You are both safe," said Abia.

Star tried to sit up and after a couple of tries she succeeded. She continued to keep her eyes closed. "Safe? We're not safe. No one on Dyanzia is safe. This is a Wardon occupied planet. How is it you haven't been captured? Wardon seized control of this planet years ago."

"There are many of us, scattered into groups that have learned to hide from the Wardons. The soldiers are very stupid and cannot catch us easily."

"How many of you are there?" she asked.

"About a thousand are left."

"A thousand?" echoed Star.

A sinking feeling came over her. All this time the Federation Chain of Life thought all the Dyanzians had been turned into slaves and all this time people had been struggling to stay free...

"Please, I need to speak with Major Hunter," said Star urgently.

Star heard Abia get up. The sound of her clothing moving indicated the woman was walking away. Soon Brianna was by her side sitting next to her. "Are you okay?" she asked.

Star shook her head. "I can't shake the dizziness, but never mind that now. We have a big problem."

Brianna snorted. "I think we have several."

Star did not mask the annoyance in her voice. "Do you know how many people are down here without mind control devices planted into their heads? A thousand! We have to rescue them – we have to get them off the planet."

Brianna was silent for a moment. "Well that really isn't our mission, is it?" she said coldly.

Star could feel a chill go up her spine. "Excuse me?"

"We're here to pick up a zombie, not rescue Dyanzians."

Despite not being able to see and her dizziness, Star instantly grabbed the young woman by the hair and pulled her off the bed and onto her knees. Brianna gasped in surprise and then yelped in pain. The move made Star feel sick, but she was too mad to care. Star pulled the young woman close as she spoke through gritted teeth. "I say our mission has changed to include saving these people, is that clear?"

Star let go of Brianna's hair and sat back on the bed. Her eyes were closed and she could hear Brianna's feet shuffle as she got up from the ground. The pain of nearly having her hair yanked out of her skull was apparent in her voice. "Well how do you think we're going to squeeze 1,000 people onto our little, and oh yeah broken by the way, shuttle?"

Star sat up straight and took a deep breath. "We can still complete the original mission, Brianna. We'll need Federation Defense to come in with a battle cruiser and transport. We will have to evacuate them."

"Oh my God, you've hit your head so hard, you've gone nuts," said Brianna. "Once my father has the Dyanzian, he's not going to come back here."

"My team will come. If I stay here."

Star could hear Brianna take in a quick breath. "You're not staying here. You're hurt and need medical attention."

"That will give my team incentive to hurry and rescue me," said Star.

Brianna shook her head. "No, you have to come with me. They won't believe I didn't kill you and then they'll kill *me*."

Star had enough. Her face turned red and her eyes, though useless to her now, blazed with rage. "I am your commanding officer on this mission –I order you to obey me!"

Brianna stopped talking. Star heard her footsteps approach her.

"How? How am I supposed to do this?" Brianna blurted out in frustration.

Star suddenly felt weak. She closed her eyes and swayed on the bed. She braced herself against the wall. "Bring in the two Dyanzians. We're going to need their help."

Brianna did what she was told and soon Star revealed to the two Dyanzians the real reason they were there. She also told them her plan to get Federation Defense to come and rescue everyone. The Dyanzians were hesitant at first, but quickly became excited about the prospects of escaping the planet and saving their friends and loved ones from the mind control.

"I am Tarek. The Wardons did not find your shuttle. My men camouflaged it before they arrived. As we've said before, they are very stupid," said the man who carried Star to safety.

"Is the Dyanzian we captured still inside the ship?" asked Star.

"Yes. In their haste, my men did not take the time to extract him. He made no noise, so they believed he was dead."

"We need help fixing the shuttle," said Star. "Is there anything you can do to help us? I still can't open my eyes without everything spinning."

"Yes," said Tarek. "We can help. Some of our older men were engineers before the invasion. They can look at your shuttle."

"I'm great with tank engines," Brianna piped in. "I can help fix the ship if you have tools."

Tarek nodded. "Yes, we have tools."

Star squeezed her eyes and shook her head back and forth to focus her sight. The effort caused her to feel faint and she fell off the bed. Abia picked her up and sat her on the bed. Star could hear the anxious tone in her voice. "Do you really think you can help the cursed? Can you bring them back to us?"

The Pente Force commander's expression went grave. "I don't know. The doctor who wants to try is a friend and he has already discovered so many wonderful cures and medicines. If anyone can find a way, he can. But

I can't promise you it will happen. I can only promise you we will try."

Brianna and Tarek disappeared out of the hut. Abia turned to Star and tried to gently push her to lie down. "You must rest," she said.

Star pushed Abia's hand a way. "You need to go with Brianna back to the ship as proof your people are still alive and without mind control devices," said Star.

Abia shook her head. "I will not leave my people. Tarek will go."

Star realized Abia was not going to budge on the subject. Star admired it – she would never leave her team in a crisis. Ever. "Then it is crucial I speak with him before they leave. There is something important I need to tell him."

"It will take time to repair the ship. You will rest until they come back. You are very seriously hurt," said Abia as she pushed Star to lie down with a firmer hand.

Star could feel exhaustion take over. The stress of the mission, the crash and escaping from the enemy were finally taking their toll. "I'm a fast healer. I will be fine," said Star allowing herself to lie down and closed her eyes. She felt a blanket cover her before she fell asleep.

***

It seemed like she was only asleep a moment when Tarek and Brianna returned. Star woke when she heard Brianna rush into the hut. Star instinctively jumped to her feet. The dizziness returned quickly as did the pain in her head. She sat back down. "Star, it's done. The damage wasn't as bad as we feared. The engineers were amazing."

"The captured Dyanzian?"

"Still in the cage. He's just fine."

Star nodded. "You have to go. Tarek will go with you. I'll stay here and help the other Dyanzians prepare to evacuate."

Brianna gave out a frustrated sigh. "You should come, too. Tarek will be proof enough there are Dyanzians here who need help."

"No. That's not how it works. I'm insurance. Mr. Sanderson will not allow the Dyanzians to continue to live like this and he won't allow your father to abandon me here. He'll back my team's efforts to rescue me and evacuate the others."

"How do you know? Your team isn't even on the HORIZON."

"I know when they find out where I've gone, they will head for the HORIZON. Listen, this is very important. You need to tell Osto the stove will only cook one egg."

Star couldn't see it, but Brianna stared at her with an unbelieving expression. Her voice gave Star a clue of how she was feeling. "You want me to tell him what?"

"You heard me."

"What does that even mean?"

"Osto will know. Now leave. I need to speak with Tarek."

Star opened her eyes and could see Brianna salute and leave the hut. Star slowly got up from the bed and poked her head out the door. Through her blurry vision she could see Tarek speaking with Abia. The night was crisp and cool and the three moons of Dyanzia hung low and full in the clear sky. Star walked towards the two giants – both stood a typical Dyanzian height and had cobalt-blue skin and smooth, bald heads. They smiled as they saw her walk toward them, but Star did not smile back.

"Tarek, after you arrive on the HORIZON, my team, the Pente Force will arrive after you. They will be angry I am not with you. Brianna will tell them why I am here and they will probably not believe her. She will tell them something and even with that they may not believe her."

"Why? Are you not fighting for the same cause? Why would they not believe her?"

"They will think she left me down here to die."

"Why would she do that?"

"Because she hates me."

"I'm confused. You both seem to care for each other's welfare. I see no hate. What could you have done to make her hate you so much?" asked Abia.

The question -- coming from a stranger -- made Star uncomfortable. It was something she was made to confess many times over the past five years, but to say it now made her heart ache. "Because I killed her sister."

Abia's and Tarek's eyes went wide. "She had a mind control device placed inside her, just like your people. I had no choice and it has haunted me ever since. That's why it is so important for us to finish this mission and try to find a cure. It's just as important to save the rest of you. Tarek, you must look to my teammate Pia and say, 'moonshine.'"

Tarek nodded. Soon after he and Brianna left. Brianna left her weapon with Star as added protection. Through periods of dizziness, Star watched the shuttle take off in the distance. As the lights from the engine disappeared into the night, Star suddenly felt as if she were trapped.

Mind Games – Part 2

Star raced through the woods, tripping over rocks in the dark and getting back up again as fast as she could. Twigs slashed at her legs when she got too close to bushes. She cursed herself, both because of the pain and the noise the small branches made betraying her position. She could hear the massive horde of mind-controlled Dyanzian zombies closing in on her. Normally, she would have been able to outrun her pursuers easily, but Star's head throbbed from a serious head injury she sustained in a shuttle crash two weeks ago. Nausea crept up from her stomach as she ran. Bile desperately wanted to escape through her mouth. Panic and anger washed over her all at once. She had no time to be sick, but she couldn't control it. She jumped behind a large nearby boulder and allowed her body to convulse. She tried to be as quiet as she could, but small noises escaped despite her best efforts. Very little fluid exited her system – she had practically nothing to eat all day. She had been hunting with some of the other fugitive Dyanzians when the Wardon-controlled zombies caught them by surprise. She still had the bodies of several medium-sized rabbit-like creatures in her backpack. Everyone ran in different directions to try to escape and she found herself cut off. If any of them made it, they knew where to rendezvous. She hated running away. She would have preferred to stand and fight, but her weak condition wouldn't allow it. Running away made her feel like a failure.

After she finished being sick, she continued to run. The sound of fast but shuffling feet and incomprehensible moans and groans seemed much louder now. Star's heart slammed against her chest and her breathing turned into labored panting. She would not be able to outrun the moaning circle of zombies closing around her. She either had to find a place to hide or go down fighting. Exhaustion slowed her pace. As she ran, she frantically searched the floor of the woods for a stick large enough to try to beat the Dyanzians back. She didn't even know how many were pursuing her or how many followed the others. She could hear the groans all around her grow louder. Maybe if there were only a couple she could fight them off. She hoped more than she believed it to be true.

Star spotted a stick she thought large enough to use against the Dyanzians near a large tree. She bent down to pick it up and a wave of dizziness overtook her. She dropped to her knees as the woods around her spun. She let go of the branch and felt herself begin to fall to the ground. Suddenly she felt a pair of large, strong hands grab her before her head could hit the ground. Sick as she felt, Star started to fight, but stopped when she heard the male voice behind her tell her to stop. The hands that grabbed her did not try to tear her apart. They belonged to a free Dyanzian. She immediately became quiet and let the man pull her up and over his shoulder and let him run with her through the woods. Star kept her eyes closed so the spinning would subside. She heard other footsteps running alongside. "I didn't see any of the others," said a woman to Star's left in her native Dyanzian.

"If they could escape, they know where to meet us," said the man carrying Star.

Star felt the man jump over bushes and boulders. He ran with her on his shoulder as if she weighed nothing at all. The jarring run caused her head to hurt and she tried unsuccessfully to suppress a grunt with every leap.

After a while, the group stopped. The man took Star off his shoulder and tried to stand her up. "We've lost them," he said to her in broken Universal.

The spinning in Star's head increased, but she opened her eyes to see a familiar face. "Blalk," she managed before everything went dark.

***

Star woke to the feeling of a cool cloth on her head. She saw the tribe elder Abia peering down on her. "Your injury still makes you weak," she said.

Star frowned. "This is the second time I've been carried like a doll," she complained.

Abia raised an eyebrow. "This is the second time you've gotten yourself into a situation where you needed to be carried."

The Special Forces commander dropped the discussion.

"Did the others come back?" Star asked.

Her barely audible voice caused Abia to sit back and glance over to the door of the treehouse where they brought Star. "All but two," she answered. "I am waiting to hear of their fate. Another rescue team went out to try to find them. The rest of the group said many of the cursed that did not go after you went after those two while the rest escaped."

Star bit her lip and closed her eyes tightly. Star didn't want to think about what would happen if Dyanzian zombies caught them. Abia leaned forward on the bed. "You can't continue to go out on hunting runs, Star," she said. "You need to heal. The injury you sustained would have killed even a Dyanzian. I don't know how you survived. If you don't rest, there's no guarantee you will continue to live."

Star opened her eyes. The dizziness began to pass and she could see Abia's weather worn face more clearly. "I need to contribute. I can't just lay here and mooch off everyone," she said.

Abia gave her a small smile and squeezed her leg. "The animals you were able to bring back will feed us tonight," she said.

Star frowned. "The others had more."

"We will work with what we have," said Abia. "We will continue to work with what we have."

Star took a deep breath. "My team will be coming," she said. "We'll all get off Dyanzia once they bring the transport."

Abia tilted her head and flashed Star a doubtful expression. "Star, it's been two weeks," she said. "Don't you think they would have come by now."

Star shook her head. "My team was not on the ship that brought me here. It will take them a while to come with a transport. The ship I was on didn't have one. I'm sure we'll hear from them soon."

"What if Brianna killed Tarek and didn't tell her father that you are alive?" asked Abia.

Star's eyes narrowed slightly. "No, despite what has happened, I trust her. She told her father. My team will come."

"How can you be so sure?"

Star gazed up at the ceiling of the hut as if she could see the stars. "They always come for me."

Blalk entered the treehouse and gave a slight bow to Abia. She rose off the bed and approached him. "Maulron and Frall were captured," he said. "The rescue party could not get to them in time. They've been taken to the factory."

Star sat up straight in the bed with such force that Abia and Blalk stopped speaking and turned to her with surprised expressions. "Wait, what? What factory?"

"The factory is where the Wardons manufacture the mind control devices," said Blalk. "It is where they turn us."

Star's face reddened. "Are you kidding me? You know why I'm here and this whole time you never said a word about it! Why?"

Abia lowered her head slightly to avoid Star's angry gaze as she approached the bed. "Star, we were going to tell you when you got better, or when help came, whichever came first," she said. "Neither did."

"I have to do something," said Star beginning to rise out of the bed. "I can't just sit here!"

Blalk's eyes narrowed and his expression turned angry. "You will do nothing! We have no weapons, no way of going up against the Wardon Empire. You will get yourself and others who follow you killed! And when you fail, the soldiers will double their efforts to come after us. We'll all be dead."

"What about Maulron and Frall? What about others that are in that factory? I have to help them!"

Abia shook her head. "Those who enter the factory come out turned," she said. "There is no hope for them."

Star stood up. The dizziness was gone. "You would give up on them so quickly?"

"There is no choice," said Blalk. "Our only hope is they don't give away our secrets through torture. As it is, we need to move camp again so as not to be discovered."

Star's voice became firm. "There's always a choice," she said.

"Not for us and until you heal completely, not for you," said Abia, her voice equally firm.

"No more talk of rescues or suicide missions," said Blalk. "We make preparations to leave."

Blalk turned his attention to Abia, who nodded, authorizing him to begin the move.

***

Osto stood on the deck of the ship JACK OF ALL TRADES, trying to mentally will the ship to go faster. He kicked the control panel in frustration and turned to his teammate. "This is ridiculous! Nine, can't you pilot this thing and make it go faster?"

Nine turned to Osto as if he were waking from a trance. "No, Osto," he said as calmly as he could. "This is a big ship and it's very old. It's going as fast as it can."

Osto let out an angry breath. "We should have brought the LIONEX. We would have been there last week," he said.

Nine had been over this with his teammate and brother for days now. Every hour Osto grew more anxious as did he. But Nine knew ships and he knew the captain of the private transport was doing her best to get them to the HORIZON. "The LIONEX only holds about 15 to 20 people packed, Osto. There are over a thousand on Dyanzia," he said.

"I know that! We could have gotten Star and then come back with this crate," he said.

Osto began to pace the floor of the main deck, swearing under his breath, stressing out his team and making the ship's crew nervous. Nine took his arm as he passed by and pulled him close. He spoke softly, but firmly. "She wouldn't have left them. You know that. That's

71

why she stayed on the planet – to make sure we would come for them all."

Osto glared at Nine, yanked his arm free and responded through gritted teeth. "She's on that planet because that witch left her there!" he hissed. "She was hurt and Brianna just left her there."

Osto paced the main deck of the lumbering ship. "We should have a Federation Defense transport," he said.

Nine's heavy sigh illustrated his frustration. "Again, Osto, they are all being used to evacuate Bopra before it's covered in lava."

Osto grunted in frustration. Hot tempered to begin with, he was beside himself with fury over Star's perceived abandonment. He was not only working himself up, he was upsetting the others. Neptune joined the conversation to try to calm him down. "Brianna gave the code and General Hunter spoke with Mr. Sanderson himself to formulate a rescue mission," said Neptune. "They are still honorable and faithful

Federation soldiers. Brianna would not have left Star or any soldier on a hostile planet unless she was ordered to do so."

Osto grew tired of arguing. It didn't make him feel better. If anything, it made him angrier. How dare Brianna abandon his sister on that planet? He turned to find Pia who was sitting with Charlie Baker, head of the Federation Knights, staring out of the large window. Charlie held one hand trying to reassure her as she silently chewed the nails of the other.

Charlie and an entire regiment of Knights came to level any Wardon bases, towers or structures they could find to create a distraction for the Dyanzian extraction. Charlie himself would take some Knights and provide cover to ensure Star and the others got out safe. Osto approached Pia and put a hand on her shoulder. "How are you doing?" he asked.

Pia stopped chewing her nails and lifted her head up. Pia's face turned pink. "If anything has happened to Star, I get to shoot Brianna," she said.

Her voice held a dead calm, her big hazel-green eyes seemed soulless. Osto understood completely. Osto loved when Pia turned cold blooded. It served them well so many times in the past. "Sure, Pia," he said, doubting it would come to it.

Pia continued her stare. "Right between the eyes, Osto," she said.

"Is there any other way?" he asked, patting her on the shoulder.

Charlie remained silent during the exchange, but shot Osto a, "you're not helping me," glance. Osto nodded at Charlie and resumed his position next to Nine.

The pilot began punching buttons and mumbling something he couldn't hear into his headset. He finally turned to the captain of the transport. "Ma'am, we are approaching the

HORIZON," he said formally and loud enough for Osto to hear.

"Finally!" said Osto.

Osto, the Pente Force and Charlie didn't stand around to wait for the Captain's formal confirmation. They headed to their cabins to get ready to meet with General Hunter and his daughter.

***

The reception the Pente Force and Charlie received aboard the HORIZON seemed chilly at best. Osto expected nothing less, nor did he care. The Hunters had been dear friends, almost like family, until Tessa Hunter's capture by Wardon. The enemy inserted a mind control device into her head and she tried to kill Star. Osto mourned Tessa when it happened, but he never understood why everyone blamed Star. She had no choice – why couldn't they see that?

The Pente Force and Charlie met with General Hunter, Brianna and Dr. Jared Thomas in the situation room. Osto opened the door and entered. The immediate tension in the room came from both sides. General Hunter and his party stood up as they entered. Osto and his team saluted. "Sit," said General Hunter.

Osto, Charlie and the team took their seats. Osto shot an angry glance Jared's way. Jared stared Osto in the eye, but could not hold it. He knew Osto blamed him partly for what happened. "Osto, here is the situation as it stands," said General Hunter as he pressed a button that turned on the map of Dyanzia.

"We last tracked your commander in this area," he said, waving his hand over the map enlarging the area. "She and the group she is with move constantly so as not to be discovered by the Dyanzians under Wardons control."

"Smart," commented Charlie.

General Hunter ignored the remark. "We don't know where the other groups are, but we assume everyone is keeping close by to make extraction faster and more efficient," he said.

76

"Sir, how is Star? What's her condition?" asked Neptune. "We initially heard she received a serious head wound, but we haven't heard anything else."

Brianna and Jared exchanged glances. General Hunter cleared his throat. "We haven't communicated with her since Brianna came back with the Dyanzians. We were tracking her with the tracker in her communicator."

Pia's face reddened. "You don't even know if she's the one with the tracker," she said through clenched teeth.

Nine's jaw dropped and Osto's face reddened. "You mean you haven't had any contact with her at all? Why?"

"She's on a hostile planet, Osto," answered General Hunter. Anger coated his voice. "It belongs to Wardon. We didn't attempt to contact her because I felt it was too dangerous. What if Wardon picked up the signal? As far as we know, they don't know she's down there. As far as we know the Wardons and their slaves are trying to track down the fugitive Dyanzians that remain free on the planet. I didn't want to jeopardize her chances."

"Or you wanted her to think we had given up on her and we weren't coming," said Nine.

The general's face reddened. "Watch yourself, Son. You forget who you're talking to," he said.

Osto didn't want to delay her rescue any longer. "Okay, so she doesn't know we're here. Can we contact her now?"

"Dyanzia is still a ride from here," said General Hunter. "My advice would be to contact her just before you get close. Just enough time for she and the Dyanzians to get to the meeting point. You won't have much time before the JACK OF ALL TRADES is discovered."

Osto nodded. "Okay, let's head out then," said Osto.

As he and the team began to leave, Brianna got up. "Commander Baker, Sir, I'd like to join the rescue mission," she said.

Everyone stopped and turned around. Charlie addressed Brianna with a cool voice. "This is not my extraction, Major. It's Osto's."

Brianna turned to a furious Osto. Her eyes seemed to plead her case. "Please, Osto. I know I'm the last person you would ever want on your mission..."

"That's right you are," he spat as he turned around.

Brianna ran in front of him and blocked his way. General Hunter called her, but she ignored him. "You're right, I left her there," she said. "I won't pretend at first I was glad. I hoped she wouldn't make it out alive. But it wasn't long after we came back, I realized what an incredibly brave and selfless person she is for doing what she did. She was willing to sacrifice herself for the good of the mission and the remaining free Dyanzians."

Osto got into Brianna's face. "She is brave and selfless. That's why she deserved better than what you gave her."

"Please let me come. She saved me down there. I need to at least make sure she comes back alive."

Osto turned to his team. The meeting left them upset, he could see it on their faces. Pia gave Osto as slight nod, indicating her consent. Soon Neptune and Nine did the same. "Charlie, I guess you have an extra set of hands," he said, not looking at Brianna. "Use them well."

With that, he and the Pente Force went to make preparations for the extraction.

***

Star packed what few items she had to pretend she was participating in the move. As she gathered her things, she looked around the hut for items she could use for her attack on the factory. She would have to sneak away while the refugees went to their next hiding place.

She walked into a small room where Abia kept medical supplies. Star found several white bottles on a shelf. She opened one and took a small sniff. The liquid had a thick, white texture, but it smelled like alcohol and most likely very flammable. "Perfect," Star said as she took two of the bottles and stuffed them into her pack. She also took a roll of gauze and left the room when she heard footsteps outside.

Abia had a bag of her own and began packing clothes and bedding. When the bag was full, she grabbed another and continued. "Can I help you?" asked Star.

Abia shook her head. "No, I am well used to doing this. Are you all packed then? Good. Can you go out and tell Blalk to come in and pack the medical supplies?" she asked.

"Of course," said Star. "Abia, do you happen to have some magnets by chance? Small but strong ones?"

Abia stopped packing and turned to Star with a confused expression on her face. "Magnets? What do you want with magnets?"

Star smiled. "It's an old fashioned Terran remedy. They used to say if you put magnets on your temples you could pull away some of the dizziness. I just remembered the tale and thought it would be worth a try."

Star hated lying, but if Abia knew what she really wanted the magnets for, she would not only refuse to give them to her, but would also try to stop her. Abia's eyes narrowed and for a moment, Star didn't think Abia bought her story. She flashed an innocent smile, forcing Abia to smile back and give out a small laugh before she left the main room and went into the back. During Abia's absence, Star went through drawers and found a small knife and some flint and small pieces of wood. It all went into her pack. Star went to Abia's small pouch purse, opened it and put her communicator inside of it just as Abia returned with two quarter sized magnets. "Will these do, Silly Terran?"

Star's eyes lit up with excitement. "Oh yes. Those will be perfect. Thank you!"

Star left the hut, delivered Abia's message to Blalk and went to talk to one of the Dyanzians who went out in search of the two captured men.

It didn't take Star long to find Javan, the tall, muscular woman warrior she recognized from the rescue party. When Star approached, Javan was packing her own things to leave. "It's such a shame we have to go," said Star as she walked up to her.

Javan regarded Star as she would a child. Star was much smaller than the giant and knowing the Dyanzian's awesome strength the woman could do some serious damage to her if she chose. Javan continued with her work as she talked. "Yes, it is a shame, but if the Wardons tortured our people, they could have told our position," she said. "As a warrior, you know that moving makes sense."

"Oh of course," said Star. "And you know for sure the Wardons took them?"

"Yes, I saw them myself heading to the factory. There they will plant those small devils into their heads and then they will slowly eat their soul."

Star shook her head. "I'm so sorry. Every one that is taken makes our numbers smaller and weaker," she said. "It's best we're moving. You're right. So, I imagine we are moving away from the factory then?"

"Of course," said Javan with a frown as she placed a large hunting knife into her luggage.

"Just curious, whereabouts is this factory? I just want to make sure if I get separated from the group, I know which way not to travel," said Star.

Javan stood up from zipping one pack and picked up another. Star noticed her intricate warrior tattoos that covered both arms and her extended right hand. Javan pointed out from the porch where they stood. "It's south about five miles," she said. "You'll hear it long before you see it. Don't worry. We will protect you. Your people will come for us and we will all be safe."

Star smiled. "Yes, thank you. I'm sure they will be here soon. You have been most helpful. I'll see you on the trail."

Javan nodded as she continued to pack weapons and other machinery. Star slipped away without another word.

No one noticed Star's absence until her communicator went off in Abia's bag. The old woman took it out and a man's voice startled her. "Star, this is Osto. Do you read me?"

"This isn't Star. This is Abia, tribal elder from a small village here on Dyanzia," said Abia.

Silence hung in the air for about 10 seconds before Abia spoke again. "Hello, are you there?"

The man's voice sounded tense. "Where is Star?"

"I don't know. She was here a minute ago, but I can't find her. We are about to leave our current hideaway and I don't know where she is."

"No, don't leave," said the man. "My name is Osto and I am on Star's team. We're here with the transport to rescue you. Gather all your people. There will be a distraction and we'll begin loading everyone onto the ship. Do you understand? Whatever you do, do not leave your position. In fact, keep the communicator with you so we can track you."

Abia nodded her head even though Osto couldn't see her. "Yes, I will. I will! Oh, thank you, thank you! I will gather my people! We'll be ready."

"Good," said Osto. "By then I'm sure Star will turn up. We'll see you shortly."

Abia put the communicator in her pocket and went as fast as she could to her people who were gathering to leave. "Everyone! Everyone! They are here! They are coming to rescue us! Star's friends have finally arrived!"

A small and subdued cheer went through the crowd. "I need runners to go to the other tribes and have them all come here. Star's people have come and they have brought a transport big enough for all of us! They are going to cause a distraction so we can board safely."

Six Dyanzians volunteered to go and alert the other tribes and to bring them to their meeting place. In all the excitement, Abia had forgotten about the little Terran who would save them all until Blalk and Javan approached her. "Abia, Star is gone," he said.

Abia's smile disappeared. "What do you mean, gone?"

87

"She had a full pack and asked me questions about where the factory was," said Javan. "She told me she wanted to know so she could avoid it. I think she lied to me."

Blalk's voice took on a grim tone. "She lied to you for sure," he said.

Abia's eyes went in the direction of the factory. The communicator in her bag suddenly made sense. "She never intended to come with us. She's gone off to try to rescue the others."

"There's more. Two containers of Flasen are gone as well as some gauze," said Blalk.

"Would she try to heal those she finds with it?" asked Abia.

Javan and Blalk exchanged looks. "No, elder. She's a Special Forces Soldier. She plans to do something else."

"How long has it been since you last saw her?" asked Abia.

"About a half an hour, elder," said Javan.

"I'll gather some men and bring her back," said Blalk as he turned to leave.

"No," said Abia. "She did not ask for help. She didn't want any more people to be lost and we will not dishonor her wishes. We will tell her team where she has gone and they will go and help her."

Blalk's eyebrows raised. "Abia? Are you sure? You ordered us to protect her no matter what the cost."

Abia nodded. "I have finally learned not to stand in her way. Make sure the others are ready to move when they come. Let us pray they do not take long."

***

Star ran in the direction where Javan pointed. Five miles should have been an easy run for her, but Star found herself struggling with the pain in her head. After a while, she could hear the noise of machinery and the foul smell of smoke byproduct that came from the factory. She jogged the rest of the way to conserve her energy. She pulled out the two weapons she kept with her when Brianna and Tarek left. She checked the power. One was dead and one had half a charge left. She hoped that would be enough for what she had to do.

The Special Forces commander cautiously peeked out of some bushes surrounding the factory. To her surprise, it didn't seem as though the Wardons were guarding it at all. In a way, it made sense to Star – the Dyanzians would never attack the factory for fear of capture. Star assumed a Wardon base was located nearby the factory and could respond to any problems. She couldn't concern herself with a base right now. She needed to see if there was anyone left to rescue and then blow up the factory.

She crept around the building several times, looking for the best and most secret way in, ducking to let a moaning Dyanzian zombie shuffle past. After the fourth go around, she decided on the back door. Overgrown vegetation partially covered it, indicating to Star it wasn't a high traffic entrance. She quickly approached the door and hid in the overgrown shrubbery as she gingerly tested the door. The rusty handle gave way easily and Star opened the door a crack. Before she could step in, she heard a loud noise coming from the southern sky.

Star went back into the bushes so she could get a better look. A smile played on her lips and her heart raced when she recognized the vessel to be a large transport. Relief washed over her. The rescue team would rescue the Dyanzians. Now she needed to save those left inside the factory. She went back to the factory, opened the door and slipped inside.

***

The JACK OF ALL TRADES blocked out the Dyanzians' view of the moon as it made its descent to the surface. Before it did, its hangar doors opened in the sky, unleashing the

Federation Air Defense Force. The fighter planes peppered the sky like a large flock of birds as they headed away from the transport to the Wardon base.

When the transport landed, the doors opened again, letting out a dozen Federation Knight tanks. The Dyanzians gasped in awe of the heavily armed mechanized vehicles as they rolled out and awaited orders. After the tanks, the Pente Force, Charlie and Brianna came out on foot to greet the Dyanzians. Abia recognized Brianna immediately and went to her. Brianna gave the elder woman a warm hug and a smile. The people Brianna brought with her were not smiling however; in fact, they seemed tense and agitated. Abia watched the hangar entrance, but no one else came out. Worry washed over her face. "Where is Tarek?" she asked anxiously.

Brianna squeezed her upper arms. "He's safe aboard the HORIZON. He's waiting for you."

Abia seemed relieved. She noticed the young people beside Brianna scanning the crowd of Dyanzians and she knew who they were looking for. "Star's gone," she said before they asked her.

"Ma'am? What do you mean gone?" asked Osto.

"We tried to keep it from her, but she discovered there is a Wardon factory here on Dyanzia."

"Factory? What sort of factory?" asked Neptune.

Abia lowered her head. "A factory that makes the mind control devices. She snuck off on her own to destroy it and rescue any of our people who could still be saved."

Osto raised his head to the sky in exasperation. "Of course she did," he said.

"We didn't want her to go. She's still injured from the shuttle crash. She snuck away while we were preparing to leave. I'm so sorry.

If we knew what she was planning, we never would have let her go."

Osto regarded the elder. Abia stood two heads taller than himself, but she seemed frail with age. "We know what she's like. We don't blame you. Stubborn! Why didn't she wait?"

Pia shot Brianna a hateful stare. "She had no idea when we would be here. No one kept in contact with her."

Brianna took a step towards Pia and Pia met her with a step of her own. Both faces turned red. "You're blaming me?" asked Brianna.

"Yes! Of course I'm blaming you! This is all your fault, Bri. All of it! All these years of you and your family torturing Star when she was hurting inside almost as much as the rest of you. Your father guilted her into this! This is all your family's doing!"

Pia's body shook with rage. Neptune stepped in between the two of them. "Enough, we don't have time for this. Star's out there hurt and alone. We need to do something. Osto?"

Before Osto could give orders, Abia stepped forward. "She took Flasen with her and gauze," she said.

Osto's eyebrows went up. "What is Flasen, Ma'am?"

Blalk and the Javan came forward. "Flasen is used as an antiseptic, but it is highly flammable," said Blalk.

"Before she left, she asked me for some magnets. She said they had to be small and strong. She told me she was going to put them on her head to stop the pain. She said it was an old Terran remedy for head injuries. I suppose that was a lie as well," said Abia.

Nine and Osto turned to each other. "Sticky bombs," they said in unison.

Osto motioned to Charlie. "We're going to need a couple of your tanks to follow us to the factory. We're also going to need the smaller transport vehicle in case there are Dyanzians in there," he said.

Charlie nodded and began calling out orders. "Mech 3 through 12, go and provide ground support to the Air Defense. Do as much damage to that base as you can so we can get these people out. Do not engage the smaller structure. There are people inside. Transport 2 you are with us. I'll call for a retreat when we're ready."

The commander of the Federation Knights heard many voices respond, "Yes Sir," in his earpiece before the tanks began to move in the direction of the base. Brianna faced Osto, Nine and Charlie. "I'll take the other tank. I want to get inside that factory and get some samples of those things they put inside my sister's head."

"Stand down, Soldier," ordered Charlie.

Osto couldn't contain his anger any longer. "I am the commander of this mission, not you. You don't get to tell me what you're going to do. I tell you! Get in that tank and you take orders from Charlie. You are to cover us while we find Star and the others. If you so much as poke your head out of that tank, I'll have Pia take it off in one shot. Am I clear?"

Brianna seemed as if she wanted to say more. She glanced at Pia who shot her a hateful glare and then to Charlie. "Yes Sir," she said finally as she boarded her tank and awaited orders.

Osto turned to his team. "Get in Charlie's tank," he ordered. "Let's go get her."

Blalk and Javan stepped forward. "We should go with you," said Blalk. "We have been caring for her since she arrived. We feel responsible that she was able to leave unattended."

Osto looked up at the two warriors and shook his head. "No, we're her team and we will be going after her. We sincerely appreciate everything you've done for Star, but now it's our turn. You have been through enough and we don't want to risk any more of you. I need you to help getting everyone onto the transport."

Blalk and Javan reluctantly agreed. "I will go and make them board faster," said Javan leaving the two men. Blalk took a deep breath and looked in the direction of the factory. "She should not have gone alone. She is still injured and is weak, but she is also brave. She is a great warrior and I hope to see her again."

Osto patted Blalk on his massive arm. "Don't worry, you will."

Osto left Blalk to help Javan get people on the transport. Abia had already taken a seat on the ship at Javan's urging. Before he went to the tank, Osto ordered several Knights to coordinate with Blalk and Javan to help get their people on board the transport faster. He told them to reassure the warriors there would be people in the hangar waiting to help them and prepare them for departure. With that, Osto climbed into the tank and it began to roll toward the factory. Dyanzian zombies, hearing the noise, came out from the dark. Abia sat in the transport, closed her eyes and prayed as the Federation Knights began to fire on them.

***

Star hid in shadows and dodged behind large objects as she explored the factory. The dank air in the facility smelled of preservatives. She waited for a Wardon scientist in a dark green coat to go past her before she opened the door to a room and poked her head in. When she discovered it was empty, she stepped in and locked the door behind her. She squinted in the dim light as her eyes adjusted. She found a light switch and flipped it on. The room held several large steel vats in the center of the room. Pipes and wires protruded from the vats, hooking them up to computers and monitors. Star walked over to the computer and took in a quick breath. She read the screen and the output of information scrolling through. Vital signs. The vats contained something or someone in each.

Star cautiously approached one of the vats. Grasping her laser tight in her hand, she opened the lid. Brown liquid filled the vessel half way. Small, white, worm-like creatures crowded inside the liquid, swimming to the top when they sensed the lid opening. Star quickly let go of the lid, letting it slam shut and preventing any of the creatures from getting out. "Oh my God," she said. "That's them. Those are the things they use to control people," she said to herself.

Star returned to the computers and studied the buttons and commands. She used the keyboard to find the menu to the program and scrolled through the options. To her surprise, she found a termination option in the menu. She glanced back at the vats. She needed to press that button. She needed to kill those things before they could hurt anyone else. Star closed her eyes and took a deep breath. What if taking some samples would help Jared find a solution to the mind control? What if the Dyanzian zombie they brought back wasn't enough? In her heart, Star wanted to kill them all for the destruction they caused, for the lives they have ruined, to include her own. Duty wanted, demanded, something else. She knew the right thing to do, as much as she hated it. She searched the drawers underneath a large table and found a container that would easily fit into her backpack. She also found a scoop she could use to get the creatures into the container without the risk of any of them getting on her.

Star lifted the lid as fast as she could and scooped out some of the creatures and some liquid. She poured them into the container. Star made sure the seal on the container was tight before she put it in the front pouch of her backpack. When she felt confident her specimens were secure, she turned back to the computer and pressed the termination button.

The humming noise that once came from the vats stopped. A red liquid filtered through a large clear pipe connected to both vats and went into the liquid containing the creatures. Star did not stay to listen to see if the horrid things made any noise when they died. She needed to find the prisoners. She opened the door, peeked outside to make sure no one was coming, and merged back into the shadows of the halls.

Alarms began sounding throughout the factory. Star let out a long, relieved breath – her team had arrived. Wardons in dark green coats ran from all different rooms and headed in the same direction, presumably to escape the invasion.

The fleeing Wardon scientists made her job much easier. She didn't have to worry about draining her laser killing them. Still, she had to act quickly. Wardon Soldiers would show up at some point to protect the factory. She heard explosions in the distance as Federation Defense attacked what had to be the nearby base. Star smiled to herself. Well, they were probably a little busy right now...

Star continued to enter rooms, killing whatever creatures she found in vats. Although she took pleasure in killing the vile little worms, she became increasingly anxious with every opened door that did not contain Dyanzians.

She walked to the end of the factory and found a door leading to a stairwell. She looked back to see if any Wardon scientists were going to head her way, but only saw a few scattered Wardons running for cover. *There must be some sort of shelter or exit there*, she thought.

Star opened the door ajar and listened for activity. After a couple of seconds, she decided it was safe and proceeded into the stairwell. She could go up or down. Star guessed she would find a bunch of scared Wardon scientists on the lower level, so she decided to see what the upper level would yield. She carefully, but quickly went up the stairs. She put her back against the wall next to the door leading out of the stairwell and listened for any noises. She cautiously opened the door and listened again. Convinced she was safe to proceed, she entered.

The second floor was one large, open area. Giant steel cylinders lined the entire floor. Star felt a chill run through her body. She knew she found the main mind control manufacturing area. She cautiously walked through, keeping close to the cylinders in case she had to duck behind one of them. She stopped at the third one in to take a closer look. She read the screen on the computer connected to it. As she suspected, it contained more mature creatures ready for insertion into victims. Star studied the room. Each cylinder contained hundreds of thousands of them. She took in a shaky breath. This facility could not continue to stand.

Then she saw them. She held her breath and went to the center of the room. Strapped to standing steel boards were the Dyanzians. About a dozen of them. None of them saw her approach. Their eyes appeared closed, either in sleep or from drugs. She cautiously approached the closest one, a young male, and touched his hand. It was Maulron, one of the Dyanzians she was hunting with when the Dyanzians attacked her group. He opened his eyes and gasped when he saw her. "Shhh. Are you infected? Did they do anything to you?" she asked quietly.

Maulron shook his head. "They were preparing us for the morning," he said. "They called us the morning batch."

Star felt her rage burn her cheeks. "Did they do any of you yesterday? Was there a batch of you yesterday? How often do they take you?"

Tears welled up in the young man's eyes. "They take a bunch of us every day. The others have already been infected and set out into the forests. We are the last."

Star nodded. "Okay, I'm going to get you out of this. I can lead you to the front of the factory, but you're going to have to get out yourselves. There is a Federation transport here that will take you and your people off the planet. Do you understand?"

Still dazed but able to understand her, Maulron nodded. Star studied the shackles. "Do you know if they left keys?"

The Dyanzian nodded. "Yes, they are over there in the second drawer," he said, trying to point with his head.

Star's eyes went in the direction of a large desk with drawers. She ran to it, pulled out the second drawer and found the keys. Other Dyanzians, to include Frall, the other Dyanzian in her hunting party, woke up when they heard the noise she made and began to chatter loudly. Star came back with the keys and addressed the prisoners. "Shhh! You must be quiet! The scientists are downstairs and I don't know for how long. If they hear you and there are soldiers in the factory, they will bring them."

She unshackled the first man and continued to work down the line as she gave out instructions. "When you're released, gather by the door. Don't open it until I tell you to. I need to make sure it's still safe."

After about 10 minutes they were all free. Star walked toward the door when she felt a sharp pain in her head. She stumbled and caught herself on one of the cylinders. Frall approached her, concern on his face. "Are you all right?"

Star shook her head to try to get the pain to stop, but it didn't. "Yes," she lied. "I'm fine. Let's get you out of here."

The Special Forces commander struggled to the door and opened it ajar. When she saw all was clear, she led the group out into the stairwell. Again, she peered down the bottom to check to see if was safe before she let anyone out. She gave the all clear. "I'm going to run and I want you to follow me," she called as she began to dart out of the door.

The Dyanzians kept close to her as she sprinted through the hallways of the first level. Just as they reached the lobby, several Wardon soldiers appeared. To make matters worse, the room began to spin. "No! Not now!" Star whispered to herself.

The Wardons fired at the group, barely missing Star and hitting the wall behind her. She pulled out her laser and stood in front of the group. "Run, run now! There are only three of them. I'll cover you. Go!"

The prisoners began to stampede towards the entrance to the factory. Star fired on the Wardon soldiers, but the spinning in her head increased. She had a hard time finding her target, but continued to fire on the humanoid objects that spun in front of her.

Star tried her best to focus and steady her hand. She continued to fire in the direction of the Wardons, while at the same time making sure all the Dyanzians got out of the lobby and to freedom. One of the Wardon shots ricochet off the wall and hit her foot. She let out a scream and fell to the floor. She lay motionless on the ground with her laser underneath her.

She could hear the soldiers cautiously approach. All they could see was her feet motionless on the floor in the prone position. "I got her!" she heard one of them say in Wardonese.

"We need to collect those Dyanzians," said another. "Lord Tozar will not be happy if any of his slaves get away."

When the three got close enough, Star jumped up and fired her weapon. The bursts killed the surprised Wardons, but it also drained her weapon. The effort also caused the pain in her head and the dizziness to increase. She fell to her knees and put both hands on her head. She couldn't make it stop. She had to make it stop. She needed to finish. Star closed her eyes and reached for one of the Wardon's weapons. She picked it up and tried to get on her feet. After two tries, she successfully got up. Her foot burned, but she was able to put weight on it. Star headed towards the stairwell. As she passed one of the doors with the now dead worms, she backtracked, went inside, and took one of the computers attached to a vat. She sat on the floor and shoved it inside her backpack. She also took out the bottles of Flasen. She opened the containers and placed a magnet in each one. With a knife, she poked holes in the caps large enough to insert some gauze that went into the liquid and left a tail on the outside. She put the lids back on the containers and sealed them tight. She used the wall to get herself back up to her feet and stumbled out of the room. She did not follow the Dyanzians out of the factory.

***

It didn't take long for the two Federation tanks to reach the Wardon factory, but to Osto it seemed like an eternity. "Come on Man, let's move this thing!" he yelled at Charlie from the back.

Charlie remained silent, but Nine shot Osto an annoyed glance. "We're going as fast as we can, Osto. Relax, we're almost there."

Osto's breath came out in quick short bursts. He balled his hands impatiently throughout the entire trip. Relaxing while his seriously injured commander was taking on an entire factory alone was nowhere near the realm of possibility for him. "I could run faster than this! We need to get there."

"He's doing the best he can, Osto," reasoned Neptune. "We are all stressed out."

Pia passed the minutes by checking her Ks-99 laser. When there was nothing left to check she turned her attention to Osto. "I'm ready," she said flatly. "What's the plan?"

"Shoot up the place and find Star."

Pia nodded slowly, her eyes fixed on him. "Awesome. Let's do this."

"Wait, that's the plan, Osto?" asked Nine.

"Look, we don't have a floor plan of the factory, so we don't know where we're going. We've got to hope most the Wardon Soldiers are busy fighting Air Defense and the Knights. I just want to get in, get her and get out. And I DON'T want Brianna getting out of the tank to go exploring. I wish you sent her to attack the base, Charlie. She's going to be a liability."

Charlie finally spoke, his voice thick with anger. "She's one of the best we have, Osto," he said. "She'll do her duty, don't worry."

"She better."

Charlie slowed the tank until it finally stopped. "We're here."

Osto frowned. "Why'd you stop?" asked Osto.

"I just said we're here."

"No. Go through the front," Osto ordered.

Charlie raised his eyebrows. "You want me to plow through the front?"

"Yes, I want you to plow through the front. This is a tank, isn't it? I need the fire power INSIDE the factory in case there's any heavy duty fighting to be done."

"Yes, Sir," said Charlie as he started the tank up again. "Knight Two, this is Knight One, we're going through the factory. Stay on my tail and wait for further orders."

"Yes, Sir," answered Brianna.

"I want the transports to stay out here…" began Charlie.

"Charlie, wait!" shouted Nine as he leaned out of his seat and looked out the window. "Stand down. There are civilians coming out of the factory!"

Osto quickly unbuckled his harness. The others followed his lead. He tried to open the back of the tank, but when he couldn't get it to open, he began banging his hands hard on it in frustration. "Get me out of here," he demanded.

Charlie came back and pressed the code to open the back. Osto jumped out and began running towards the fleeing Dyanzians. "Hey, over here! We're here to rescue you. Come this way!" he yelled.

The Pente Force and Charlie were close behind him. Maulron approached Osto. His eyes were wide with fear and his breathing labored. "There's a fire fight. The girl is alone with only one laser. She set us free and told us to run!"

Brianna joined the group. Osto patted the man on the arm and pointed toward the transport and told the man and the others to run toward it. Osto then bolted for the entrance, his team, Charlie and Brianna behind him. They rushed into the lobby. Osto saw the Wardon bodies and led the group in their direction. He stood over them for a moment and noticed Star's Ks-99 on the ground. He picked it up and quickly examined it. "It's dead," he said.

He examined the ground where the three bodies lay. He only saw two guns. "She's armed with one of theirs," he said.

"Where do you think she is?" asked Charlie.

Before Osto could voice his guess, gun fire came from behind him. Wardon soldiers had

THE PENTE FORCE CHRONICLES MIND GAMES

come up from another entrance and began to attack.

Laser fire bombarded the group. Pia jumped up on a pile of crates giving her a good vantage point over the enemy. She began a slow steady stream of her own laser fire.

Suddenly a Wardon soldier charged the group and threw a grenade at Osto and Nine. The two Special Forces Soldiers didn't move. They were too distracted with their fight to see what the Wardon had thrown at them. Charlie yelled for them to move, but they didn't appear to hear him. Brianna was closest to them and she knew time was running out. She charged for the grenade, diving for it in an attempt to reach it and avoid the laser fire above her. She grabbed the small bomb and threw it back as hard as she could. The move exposed her arm to laser fire and she caught a blast just above her wrist. She yelped in pain as she covered her head in anticipation of the explosion.

Osto and Nine stared at Brianna in disbelief. They didn't have time to pull her back with them as they ducked and awaited the blast. The explosion rocked the lobby, killing some of the Wardon soldiers and sending debris raining down on the Special Forces team. Charlie ran to Brianna and pulled some gauze out of his utility belt to address the wound. "I'm fine," she winced as he bound her bleeding arm.

"Yeah, sure you are," he said.

More enemy soldiers came through the smoke, firing lasers. Dyanzian zombies, growling and drooling, accompanied them.

Osto swore under his breath. There were too many of them to fight exposed in the lobby. He had to make sure the refugees were safe before he could find Star. "Get back to the tanks!" He ordered.

Pia, who had been firing calmly and steadily into the crowd of Wardons immediately protested. "What? Why? We're doing fine. We need to find Star."

"Get back to the tanks! We need to make sure the prisoners are safe. We'll have better luck fighting the Wardons with the tanks' fire power," he said as he grabbed Pia's and Brianna's arms in retreat.

The group ran out of the factory. Everyone except Osto climbed back into their tanks. He ran to the transport. The Federation Knights driving the vehicles had just finished loading up the last of the prisoners. Osto flailed his arms wildly at the drivers. "Get them out of here! We're under attack! We're going back in to find Star. Get them to safety."

The Knights saluted and jumped into the transport and left with the prisoners. Osto returned to Charlie's tank and closed the back. "Punch it!" He ordered. "Get in there!"

Charlie moved the tank and proceeded to go back through the factory entrance.

***

After what seemed like a lifetime, Star made it back to the second floor. She had to stop several times and vomit from the spinning and the pain in her head. She went into the center of the room and took the flint and a stick out of her utility belt. She lit one of the sticky bombs and closed her eyes. She concentrated and called on her failing strength as she wound up and threw the flaming bomb at a cylinder at the far end of the room. She heard a click, indicating the magnets stuck to their target. Star closed her eyes and ran towards the entrance. She opened them again long enough to light the second one and throw it. She fled as fast as she could down the stairs. Suddenly she heard a loud noise that sounded like an explosion in the lobby. The building shook throwing her from the last few stairs to the ground. Star fell hard and it took her a while to get up. Knowing the entire factory was likely to go up in an explosion, she tried desperately to get out of the stairwell and back to the lobby. When she finally made it, she saw the cause of the noise. Two Federation tanks in the lobby were firing at a large group of Wardon soldiers and Dyanzian zombies. As Star approached, the last of the Wardon soldiers fell dead from the tank's firepower. Star ran towards the tanks and began waving her arms and screaming at them. "Get out! It's going to blow! Get out!"

***

Charlie had just finished firing the cannon that took down the last soldier, when Nine noticed Star running towards the tank. She fell to her knees but got back up. "Star! There's Star!" he shouted.

The occupants of the tanks cheered. Osto began to unbuckle his harness and make his way to the back of the tank when an explosion rocked the factory. He and the team looked out the window just in time to see the explosion rip through the lobby, sending Star flying towards the tank. "No, no no!" screamed Osto.

Pia and Neptune began screaming as a cloud of smoke and debris obscured their view of the commander. The dust settled enough for them to see Star in a puddle of blood in front of the tank. Charlie rushed to open the back of the tank. Osto and Nine jumped out and ran for Star. Three more Wardon soldiers came out from the other entrance and advanced towards Star. Osto and Nine were trying to get to Star before the enemy. In her own tank, Brianna had a better vantage point than Star's teammates. As the Wardons raised their weapons to fire upon the trio, Brianna carefully aimed her cannon. "No you don't," she hissed as she put her finger on the button.

With the skill of a sniper, she quickly dispatched the would-be assassins. Nine and Osto, not expecting assistance, jumped in surprise. Nine turned to Brianna's tank and nodded his thanks. Osto's attention went to the factory ceiling when he heard the creaking of support beams breaking. The ceiling began to crumble and large chunks fell all around them. Nine scooped up Star and the two ran back to their tank. Brianna opened the top of her tank and started to get out to assist with Star. Osto looked back and started yelling. "Get back in your tank. Retreat, retreat! This place is about to come down!"

Brianna quickly closed the top of her tank and hit the reverse and left the factory. Osto and Nine, with Star in his arms, jumped back into the tank and headed out as well.

As the two tanks made a hasty retreat, Osto could feel the ground rumble from the crumbling factory from where he sat. When it came down, the deafening noise traveled for miles. Neptune took Star out of Nine's arms. She took off the backpack and gave it to Pia to put on and laid Star across their laps. She put her ear to Star's mouth and heard wheezing breaths. She and Pia checked her and found rebar pierced near her left shoulder blade and in several places on her body. Bruising from the force of the blast had already began to appear on her body. Star bled everywhere. Pia tried to wipe it away with the sleeves of her uniform.

Osto held Star's hand while the two women worked. "Well?" he asked.

Neptune looked up from her work, fear in her eyes. "She needs help now, Osto. I don't know if she's going to make it. She needs to get to the HORIZON."

Charlie got on the communicator, his voice panicked. "I need a fighter jet at the rendezvous point right now! The closest one," he ordered.

A voice came through the speaker. "This is Air Defense Six," she said. "I'm landing now."

Charlie got back on the communicator. "Air Defense Six, we'll be right there."

"Copy that. Air Defense Six Out," she said.

Pia and Neptune began to compress some of Star's wounds with their hands. Osto also helped, but he didn't know what he was doing. Nine sat helpless in the front with Charlie watching the team trying to save her. He turned to Charlie. "I'm taking Air Defense Six back to the HORIZON," he said. "No one flies faster than me."

Charlie took his eyes off the road only for a moment to shoot his best friend a concerned glance. "And what if she dies on the way, Nine?" he asked. "Are you prepared to live with that?"

"Yes."

Charlie's face turned grim and his eyes returned to the road. "Okay."

The tanks returned to the refugees' hiding place. Osto jumped out of the tank first and lifted Star out of the two young women's laps. Nine quickly followed and both men ran to the waiting fighter. Horror spread on the face of the young pilot as she saw who was coming towards her. She remained speechless as Osto ran past her and began climbing up into the jet with Star on his shoulder. Nine grabbed the helmet out of her hand. "I'm taking your plane," he said over his shoulder as he climbed into the cockpit. "I'll give it back later."

"Yes, Sir," she managed as she watched Nine lower the cockpit shield. Osto strapped Star in, closed her shield and jumped off the plane. Nine was in the air in moments, flying as fast as the fighter would go to the HORIZON.

Charlie called five more fighters to take himself and the rest of the team back to the ship. If something were to happen, he knew the team would want to be there. He wanted to be there. Star was like a sister. He wanted to be there for her if it was the end. He left Brianna in charge of finishing the extraction. He ordered the tanks back to the transport and ordered Air Defense to provide cover during the retreat.

***

When Nine and Star arrived on the HORIZON, the doctors immediately rushed her into surgery. By the time she got out, everyone had returned to the ship and the HORIZON made a hasty retreat out of Wardon territory before the Wardon Empire could retaliate with more warships. While Star was in surgery, Pia

124

went through her backpack and found the computer and the sample of worms Star brought back. The container was intact and the worms inside were still alive. She handed over the materials to Jared. General Hunter and Brianna were present when Pia delivered the items. "Despite everything, she managed to get more samples and brought back information on the mind control devices," said Brianna.

"If I can extract the information from this computer, it will be invaluable to our cause," said Jared. "The larvae will help us understand how they develop."

"She did more than what we asked her to do," confirmed General Hunter.

Pia sniffed at the trio. "Enough is enough. You've got to stop doing this to her. She's paid her debt to you and then some. You need to finally make peace with what happened."

General Hunter shook his head. "No. No more. It's finished. I've been wrong to put her through that. To put all of us through that. You don't understand. None of you do. To lose a child. I was so angry. I'm sorry for taking it out on Star. I just missed my little girl so much."

Pia said nothing. After one last look at the three, she turned on her heel and left.

***

After days of uncertainty, Star came out of the coma she lapsed into due to her extensive injuries. She woke up to find a teddy bear tucked next to her with a note: "I'm sorry."

A large bouquet of flowers with a large "Thank you. The Hunters" card stood on a table at the foot of her bed. Her teammates told her of Brianna's bravery during the mission and how she saved Osto, Nine and herself. A single tear rolled down Star's cheek and she took in a deep breath. The five-year ordeal was finally over.

Weeks later Star recovered enough to transfer to Beta Control, the Federation Flagship Base on Earth to continue healing.

Federation Science and Medicine, headed by Queen Moreen of Zatoks, took over the care of the Dyanzians and treated them for injuries and malnourishment. At Abia's request, they relocated to a small planet within the safety of the Chain of Life. The Chain provided the survivors with everything they needed to rebuild their lives and civilization.

During the weeks after the mission, Jared began to extract valuable information from the computer regarding the mind control larvae. Jared discovered some disturbing revelations. The end of the mind control device project was not yet over.

Mind Games - Part 3

Neptune and Pia raced across a lake on planet Dreaon in an airboat. Neptune drove while Pia stood behind the small laser cannon attached to the boat's stern. She had trouble seeing in the dark and they hit several objects in the water as they sped towards their destination. Neptune didn't stop to see what she hit. Soon after hitting an object, she hit something else, something large. It nearly sent Pia out of the boat. "Come on!" Pia protested. "Be more careful!"

Neptune barely heard her with the sound of the engine in her ears, but Pia's tone told her all she needed to know and Neptune ignored her. She was annoyed, but not with Pia. Their childhood friend, and up and coming scientific star, Dr. Jared Thomas, had disappeared. No

129

one knew where he went until Federation Intelligence picked up a message from a Wardon warship reporting a Federation shuttle in Wardon territory. The enemy followed the shuttle to the planet and planned to capture the pilot. Lucky for Jared, the Pente Force was close enough to respond when Mr. Richard Sanderson asked them to go to Dreaon, locate him and bring him back. Neptune frowned to herself. This was so unlike Jared. He wasn't one to be reckless and fly into Wardon territory. What was he thinking?   What was he doing all the way in the Dyanzian System?

Pia tapped Neptune on her shoulder and pointed up to the sky. Neptune felt her blood run cold. A large Wardon ship sat just under the clouds above them. The ship flashed a floodlight into the water a few hundred yards away. Neptune looked towards the light and found what they were looking for. Jared sat in a small rowboat. She watched in horror as he became startled by the light and tried to row the boat through the water to get away.

Neptune grunted and pushed the accelerator pedal down as far as it would go. She saw Jared turn his head in their direction. Neptune guessed he could not see who was approaching. He doubled his attempts to escape. Neptune yelled over her shoulder to Pia. "You're going to have to try to grab him off the boat. Whatever you do, DO NOT fall out."

Pia nodded and left the laser cannon. "I've got this," she yelled.

Above them, Neptune heard laser fire. She started evasive maneuvers, but then took a moment to look up. The Wardon ship did not fire at their boat. Instead, it fired on the Pente Force's ship, the LIONEX. The ship, with Osto and Nine aboard, provided cover for Pia and Neptune so they could rescue Jared. The plan was working.

Neptune let out a loud sigh of relief and slowed the boat as much as she dared. "Get ready! Here we go!"

Pia positioned herself close to the side of the boat where she would try to scoop up Jared. She braced her feet under the seat and leaned over, her arms stretched. She might only get one shot. Neptune got close enough where Pia could grab him by his shirt and belt. Pia grunted as she yanked the young scientist off his boat and onto theirs.

Once Jared was on board, Pia returned to her laser cannon. She pushed the nose of the cannon up manually, punched a few buttons to turn it on, and then took aim. Her skills as a marksman were unsurpassed, but Pia had to be careful not to hit the LIONEX. Even with the bumps that Neptune couldn't avoid, Pia still got a few good shots in on the Wardon warship.

The ruckus Pia made with the cannon drew unwanted attention. Neptune could see laser fire coming at them; however, it didn't come from the Warship. Two other airboats sped towards them from across the lake. Neptune could see the dark green uniforms in the light provided by the warship's floodlight above them. The Wardon soldiers were on the water, presumably to capture Jared.

Neptune turned the airboat around and began to retreat. Pia opened her mouth to protest, but then she saw the laser fire coming their way and closed it. She swung the laser from the warship towards the two pursuing airboats. The ships continued to fire on them. Neptune zig-zagged around the lake to get away and to avoid the deadly laser fire. Her erratic driving caused Jared to slam into the cannon and hit Pia's foot. Neptune's frenzied attempt at escape made her miss her target. Pia hated to miss. "Drive straight!" Pia demanded as she tried to zero in on one of the other airboats.

"I can't. I'm trying to keep us alive! If I drive straight, they'll get us for sure."

"I can't get a clear shot! I can't get them at this angle," protested Pia.

Neptune zigged and a blast from the

Wardon's laser cannon hit the water just inches away from them. "Try!"

Pia huffed and stepped up onto the laser cannon itself, almost straddling it so when the boat turned, she turned with the cannon and wouldn't fall. "Jared, strap yourself in! You're ruining my shots!" she ordered.

As Jared buckled himself in, Pia took aim once again. She waited for Neptune to zag. She fired one shot. Although it wasn't the bullseye she had hoped for, she still managed to hit the side of the boat. She caused enough damage to make the enemy stop and put out the small fire caused by her blast.

Pia didn't celebrate. One other airboat pursued them. The Wardon boat fired wildly at theirs, chipping away at the sides and the back of the giant propeller next to the cannon. Pia glanced down at Jared before she aimed again. She couldn't see his face in the dark, but she saw his chest go up and down at a rapid pace and she knew he was afraid. She went back to her mission. Pia aimed at the boat and waited for Neptune to zig. When she did, Pia fired once more. This time, the other airboat caught on fire. The Wardon soldiers jumped to save themselves, firing at the Pente Force with hand lasers right up until they hit the water. Neptune sped away in search of dry land and the small ship they came in. She was anxious to get off the planet and get back to the LIONEX.

After about a 10-minute ride, Neptune located their ship and drove the boat up to the edge of the beach. When she shut off the motor, she approached Jared and unbuckled his seatbelt. Jared began to stutter. She could see the fear in his eyes. "N-Neptune, wait. I can explain why…"

Neptune removed the seatbelt, grabbed Jared by the shirt and threw him onto the beach. Pia raised her eyebrows, but gave an approving nod as the two young women jumped off the boat. Neptune picked Jared up and put him on his feet. She still had him by the shirt when she put her face up to his. "What are you doing here, Jared? What are *we* doing here, huh? Have you lost your mind? You have a Wardon warship looking for you!"

Jared's face got red and he pried Neptune's hands off his shirt. "I'm not here on vacation! I have a very good reason for being here."

Pia's face took on an angry appearance as well. "Spill," she demanded.

"It doesn't matter," said Neptune. "We're leaving. You can explain yourself to Mr. Sanderson."

"No!" said Jared. "Wait! We can't leave! I need to stay."

Neptune frowned at Jared. "Are you nuts?" she asked. "Seriously, what is wrong with you? We can't stay here. This planet is under Wardon rule. There's probably a dozen more of those boats out there looking for you and bring you back to their ship."

136

"This is where they breed them!" said Jared.

His quick breathing and wild-eyed look concerned Neptune. Pia frowned at him. "Who? Breed what? What are you talking about? We've got to get out of here."

Jared took a step toward them. "The larvae are genetically engineered by Wardon scientists. This is where they are breeding them for the mind-control devices," he explained. "They're doing it in one of the ponds on this planet. I found the map to the planet and the information on the computer Star took from the factory before she blew it up."

Pia and Neptune exchanged worried glances. "And this is something you didn't feel like sharing with Mr. Sanderson?" asked Neptune.

Jared shook his head. "No. I thought if I just came out here by myself..." he began. "I didn't think they would see one guy. I thought I could get in under their radar, destroy the

137

breeding pond, get out and put an end to this once and for all. Star is in the hospital, partly because of me. I didn't want anyone else to get hurt."

Pia's gaze went from Jared to Neptune. "Well, this isn't good."

A large explosion came from the sky in the direction where the LIONEX and the warship were battling. Neptune took in a deep breath and let it out. "No, not good at all."

"What do you want to do?" asked Pia, looking to the sky. She had a worried expression on her face. Neptune seemed worried, too. The mission was to bring Jared back, not to launch an attack on a Wardon planet. They wouldn't have a lot of time. Enemy reinforcements would be coming and soon. "Where is the pond?" asked Neptune.

"I was on my way there when everyone showed up," said Jared. "It was going to take forever in that rowboat I was in. We're going to have to go back to find that. My equipment is in that boat. Then we can head out and get to the pond."

"They have airboats too, and it's dark. We might be able to get past any that are on the lake if we don't get too close," reasoned Pia.

Neptune considered. "We should tell Osto," she said. "Maybe they could take the LIONEX out of orbit and come back for us."

Pia nodded. "He's not going to be happy," she warned.

Neptune used her communicator to talk with Osto. After much swearing and yelling, he agreed the two soldiers should help Jared destroy the breeding pond. "Okay, let's do this," she said. "Let's camouflage the shuttle so we'll have a way to get out of here."

Neptune and Pia went up to the shuttle just a few yards away from the beach. Neptune found the control panel just below the wing and opened it with a series of numbers. Once the panel opened, Neptune pressed a few more buttons and took out a small remote control from the compartment to deactivate the camouflage when they returned. In just a moment, the shuttle became part of its environment and blended in with nearby sand dunes. Neptune and Pia led Jared back to the airboat and took off. Pia took her place behind the cannon. Jared silently strapped himself in and tried not to annoy the girls any more than he already had.

Neptune circled the lake twice before they found Jared's rowboat. He climbed out of the airboat, picked up the duffle bag from the bottom and transferred it to the other. He jumped back into the airboat and Neptune took off. Jared pulled the map out of the bag and a flashlight to read it. "Hey, put the flashlight away!" yelled Pia. "We're trying not to be seen out here."

"I have to get my bearings," protested Jared. "We need to head south. We land on the beach and then start walking toward the pond."

"Don't you think they're going to have soldiers all over that pond now they know we're here?" asked Pia.

"Yes, they will," said Neptune. "We're going to have to leave the airboat at a distance and swim to shore."

"Is the duffle bag waterproof?' asked Pia. "It better be."

"It's not, but the tools I need can get wet," said Jared.

Neptune glanced at Pia and then their friend. "Jared, maybe you should stay on the boat and let us do this," she suggested. "You'll be safer here."

Jared shook his head. "No way. If the Wardons come by, I'm dead. Plus, you don't know where the pond is and you don't know how to use the chemicals I brought correctly."

Pia regarded Neptune and shook her head. "You tried," she sighed.

Neptune got the airboat as close to the shore as she could. She shut off the engine. "Okay, we're here," she said.

The three got into the water and swam the rest of the way. Jared placed the map in a plastic bag to keep it dry. Once ashore and on the beach, Pia and Neptune helped cover the flashlight as Jared looked at the map and got their bearings. Jared looked around and pointed east. "It's that way," he whispered.

"Stay behind us," whispered Neptune.

She and Pia pulled out their Ks-99 lasers and ran up the beach to the woods. Jared followed close behind. Once they made the woods, they hid behind trees as they went. They snuck past several armed Wardon Soldiers, who seemed to be looking for them. Pia and Neptune exchanged looks. Pia lifted her eyebrows and held up her laser to her chest. Neptune shook her head no. She knew Pia wanted to fight, but they had no idea how many more of the enemy they would encounter. She wanted to conserve their fire power and their energy. She also didn't want Jared to get into the cross fire. As angry as she was at him, he was a civilian and a friend, not to mention unaltered. He didn't have speed, strength or the ability to heal as they did. They had to protect him.

As expected, the closer they got to the pond, the more soldiers they saw. When they got to the edge of the pond, they hid behind a large boulder. Neptune looked out towards the pond. Dozens of Wardon soldiers surrounded it. A large filtration system sat on one of the edges of the water. Pia also surveyed the pond. "So how do you want to do this?" she asked.

"Try to get as many of them away from the pond as we can so Jared can get this done," said Neptune.

"Do you want me to go first?" Pia asked.

"Yes. I'll get the ones who don't follow you, "said Neptune.

Pia turned to Jared. Her face had a stressed, stern appearance. He hardly recognized her. "They aren't all going to follow us, Jared," she said. "They aren't that stupid. Will you be able to destroy the pond and get away? We won't be able to help you. We'll be busy with the ones that follow us."

Jared turned towards the pond and the soldiers. "I'm so sorry I got you into this," he said. "I really thought this was going to go smoother. I didn't want anyone else to be involved."

Neptune put her hand on his shoulder. "You're a scientist. This is not your job. This is ours. You should have come to us and we would have taken care of it. It's no use fighting about it now. We're here so let's do this."

Pia got up and started to leave. She patted Jared on the shoulder. "Good luck, you guys," she said.

"Good luck, Pia. The meet up spot is back at the airboat," said Neptune.

Pia nodded and disappeared into the woods. Jared took a deep breath. "Now what do we do?"

"We wait for Pia to be Pia," said Neptune.

After a few minutes, Neptune saw a bright blue ball fly towards the filtration system. Pia's orb bomb exploded, damaging the machine. The Wardon soldiers scrambled around, looking for the origin of the bomb. Pia fired her laser, killing about three of them. The Wardons returned fire. More than half of them ran after Pia, who slipped away deeper into the woods.

Neptune took in a deep breath and closed her eyes in concentration. When she opened them, she saw Jared's frightened face staring at her. "You're not going to choke now are you? This whole thing was your idea. You need to be strong."

Jared swallowed hard. He took out a container of liquid and a laser gun of his own. His hands shook as he tried to hold the weapon.

"I'll admit it. I'm scared," he said. His voice quivered when he made his confession. "How is it you're not scared when you do missions like this? I would never be able to do this."

"We are scared," said Neptune. "We overcome it because people die if we don't."

"Pia's not scared," concluded Jared. "She fights as if she was born to do it."

"Jared, she was born to do it," said Neptune. "We all were. Pia is scared, but she just channels it really well."

Neptune heard another orb bomb go off at the edge of the woods and the screams of Wardon soldiers. When only a few more soldiers ran to help, she knew it was her turn. "We're up," she said. "Wait until I get as many as I can to follow me, then sneak up and do what you can. I recommend going behind the tree that's closest to the pond and doing your work there."

Jared nodded. Neptune smiled at him. "You'll do fine. See you back at the boat."

With that Neptune snuck around the opposite way Pia went and commenced her attack. It wasn't long before Jared heard another orb bomb go off. Neptune hit the filtration system again while some of the soldiers were trying to put out the first. They died in the blast, leaving fewer for her friend to deal with. Jared began crawling to the tree where Neptune instructed him to do his work. He stopped every now and again to let a running Soldier pass him. He could feel his heart pounding in his chest and he broke out in a cold sweat whenever one of the soldiers got close. Thankfully they didn't notice him. Neptune got seven soldiers to follow her into the woods, leaving five -- far too few to guard every inch of the pond – most of who were trying to put out the destroyed filtration system.

Jared finally made his way to the tree. Smoke from the filtration fire and laser blasts filled the air close to the pond. The smoke also provided a little extra cover for Jared. He opened the receptacle containing a poison that doubled as a flammable liquid and poured it into the pond. After he emptied the contents, he ducked back behind the tree and waited. He knew it would only take a few minutes for the liquid to disperse into the pond. He knew the eggs were already dying just by having the chemicals contaminate the water. The filtration system was offline thanks to Pia and Neptune. While he waited for the chemicals to spread through the rest of the pond water, he could hear the battle going on around him. *Those two are really making a commotion*, he thought. He didn't care what Neptune said, the Pente Force were the bravest people he knew.

When he felt the time was right, Jared fired his laser into the pond. The water lit up immediately and the fire spread in seconds. As soon as he saw the flames, he ran. He knew the soldiers would try in vain to put out the fire, but he also knew some would come looking for him just as they had gone after Pia and Neptune.

Jared ran as fast as he could into the woods, keeping close to the trees for cover. He heard footsteps behind him. He ducked behind a tree and watched a Wardon soldier pass him. He took off in the opposite direction and soon he was at the edge of the water. He spun around several times and listened to see if anyone was following him or if Neptune and Pia were around. He was alone. He waded into the water as fast as he could so as not to be seen and swam to the boat, trying to be as quiet as possible. Once he reached it, he lay at the bottom and caught his breath. The adrenaline still coursed through his body. He did it. They did it. It wasn't all the eggs, but the pond was the main source. Emperor Tozar would have a hard time producing large quantities of mind-control devices now that his main factory on Dyanzia and main source of supply on this planet were gone.

As he lay in the boat, he heard a splashing sound coming from the beach area. He sat up and saw Neptune wading into the water and start swimming towards the boat. His heart leapt to see his friend, but concern quickly took over as he scanned the beach for Pia. No sign of her yet. Neptune pulled herself into the boat and sank to the bottom. Jared watched her for a moment and then his attention went back to the beach. Where was she?

"Neptune, did you see Pia?" he asked. "She was the first one of us to attack and now she's the last to come back."

Neptune sat up in the boat. Small cuts from running through the tall brush covered her face and hands, and the dirt she had on her face had either washed off or smeared into muddy patches around her cheeks and nose. "She's always the last to come back," she said. "I'm not worried yet. I'll give her a few minutes and then I'll go out after her."

"Shall I go?" offered Jared.

Neptune shot him an angry expression. "No, don't be silly," she said scornfully.

Pia had the most soldiers follow her and so it wasn't unusual for her to take longer, but after a while Neptune also began to worry. She knew this mission was in and out. Why delay? Neptune tried to play off her growing concern so Jared would not panic. "Okay, I think she's had time enough to play with the Wardons," she said as she began to get up and get back into the water. "Stay here."

Jared nodded and watched Neptune swim back to the beach and jog into the woods. She wasn't gone long. Soon she appeared with Pia. Jared's elation upon seeing his friends ended when he saw Pia stumble and Neptune drag her from the beach into the water. Jared went to the controls and turned the boat on. As they swam towards him, he got the boat up next to them. With strength he didn't know he had, he yanked Pia up by both arms and got her in the boat. After he helped Neptune onto the boat, he turned to the boat controls. Neptune grabbed him by the arm and pushed him away from the controls. "Pia needs help," she shouted as she put the boat into full throttle and raced away from the shore.

As they sped away, a few remaining soldiers appeared on the beach and began firing. But they were too far away for it to make a difference.

Jared stared down at Pia who was writhing in pain in the fetal position at the bottom of the boat. He turned her on her back and saw the entire left side of her uniform saturated in blood. He tore at her uniform just enough to see a laser wound and the blood leaking from it. A quick search of the boat turned up nothing. He left the duffle bag which contained medical supplies at the side of the pond. He pulled off his shirt and pressed it against the wound, causing Pia to scream in pain. "I'm sorry, I'm sorry," he said. "I have to stop the bleeding."

Jared yelled over the engine of the boat. "You have a first aid kit on the shuttle and medical facilities aboard the LIONEX, right?" he said.

Neptune nodded as she turned the boat to avoid the attention of a distant airboat. Jared turned back to Pia. He kept the pressure on until they got to the beach on the other side of the lake. "We're almost there," he reassured Pia.

Pia grimaced in pain and nodded. "From now on I wear my battle armor when I come looking for you," she said through gritted teeth.

Neptune and Jared got Pia onto the ship and flew back to the LIONEX. As Jared stitched Pia up, he realized that although he had completed his mission, he did so by risking his friends. He wished he could promise them that he would never leave the lab again, that he would stay safe so they didn't have to worry about him, but he couldn't. He had a taste of adventure. He had a taste of what their lives were like and he was hooked. He would try to find a way to be a part of their adventures, but that would have to wait for a while. He would need to take a break from racing around the galaxy until their anger subsided and he complete his all-important mission. They gave him everything he needed. He only had to focus on the task at hand. He had to focus on finding a way to heal those already inflicted with the Wardon mind-control device. After that, well, who knows.

About the Author

Ann Marie R. Harvie has been the editor of the award winning magazine, "The Yankee Engineer," since 1992. She is a contributing writer to the "Army Engineer Magazine" the "Corps Environment," and writes reviews for Yelp and Trip Advisor.

She has had short stories from the "Pente Force Chronicles" series published in small press magazines, blogs and anthologies over the years. She was a series author on the subscription site www.Chanillo.com.

Follow Ann Marie:

Blogger -
http://storiesfromoutofthisworld.blogspot.com

WordPress -
https://storiesfromoutofthisworld.wordpress.com

Website - www.penteforce.com.

Twitter - @EditorYE.

Facebook:
https://www.facebook.com/PenteForce

LinkedIn -
https://www.linkedin.com/in/annmarie-harvie-a65a991a